Herman Heijermans

The Ghetto

A drama in four acts

Herman Heijermans

The Ghetto
A drama in four acts

ISBN/EAN: 9783337303839

Printed in Europe, USA, Canada, Australia, Japan

Cover: Foto ©Andreas Hilbeck / pixelio.de

More available books at **www.hansebooks.com**

THE GHETTO

Plays

THE PLAYS OF HENRIK IBSEN. Small 4to, cloth,
5s. each, or paper covers, 1s. 6d. each.

JOHN GABRIEL BORKMAN.	*THE MASTER BUILDER,
LITTLE EYOLF.	*HEDDA GABLER.

* *Also a limited Large Paper Edition, 21s. net.*

BRAND : A Dramatic Poem in Five Acts. By HENRIK
IBSEN. Translated in the original metres by C. H.
HERFORD. Small 4to, cloth, 7s. 6d.

THE PLAYS OF GERHART HAUPTMANN. Paper
covers, 1s. 6d., or cloth, 2s. 6d. each.

*HANNELE.		LONELY LIVES
	THE WEAVERS.	

* Also small 4to, with Portrait, 5s.

THE PRINCESS MALEINE, and THE INTRUDER.
By MAURICE MAETERLINCK. With an Introduction
by HALL CAINE, and a Portrait of the Author. Small
4to, cloth, 5s.

THE FRUITS OF ENLIGHTENMENT : By Count
LYOF TOLSTOY. With Introduction by A. W. PINERO.
Small 4to, with Portrait, 5s.

CYRANO DE BERGERAC. By EDMOND ROSTAND.
Small 4to, 5s. Also, Popular Edition, 16mo cloth,
2s. 6d. ; paper, 1s. 6d.

———

LONDON : WILLIAM HEINEMANN
21 BEDFORD STREET, W.C.

THE GHETTO

A DRAMA

In Four Acts

Freely Adapted from the Dutch of
HERMAN HEIJERMANS, Jr.

By
CHESTER BAILEY FERNALD

LONDON: WILLIAM HEINEMANN
MDCCCXCIX

DRAMATIS PERSONÆ

RAFAEL.
SACHEL.
AARON.
RABBI HAEZER.
SAMSON.
DANIEL.
MORDECAI.
ESTHER.
REBECCA.
ROSA.

A Watchman.   Inhabitants of The Ghetto.

The action takes place in The Ghetto, Amsterdam, at the present time.

The incidental music composed by Mr. N. CLIFFORD PAGE.

PREFACE

In the not wholly grateful task of adapting this play to the present demands of the English and American stage, partly as those demands have been interpreted by others than me, numerous alterations have been thought necessary. I hope that this adaptation does not conceal the fact that Mr. Heijermans' original is a work of very admirable unity and force.

CHESTER B. FERNALD.

September, 1899.

THE GHETTO

THE FIRST ACT

SCENE: *A street in the Ghetto in Amsterdam. On the left the shop of* SACHEL. *Running down from the centre to the right, diagonally, the wall of a canal; a bridge across the canal; a vista of the river and the city at the back.*

Enter SAMSON *and* DANIEL.

SAMSON.

Have trade and traffic gone to bed for Sabbath?

DANIEL.

Not till old Sachel shuts his shop. See, he sits there in the gloom like a spider waiting in its web. He would keep open all night for two cents.

A

SAMSON.

He's waiting for his son. What if the old man knew that Rafael spent half his time composing music—music for which he gets nothing? He would lock the door on Rafael to-night.

DANIEL.

Let him! The world shall hear from Rafael. Wait till we play his music.

SAMSON.

But he still has time to devote to his father's Christian servant-maid.

DANIEL.

Eh—you have noticed too? [*They look into the shop.*] Ah, see her! I say, she's the handsomest in Amsterdam—high or low! You had better be careful what you say about her to Rafael.

SAMSON.

I am. When I spoke a trifle lightly of her, he offered to smash my head with your 'cello.

DANIEL.
And you apologised?

SAMSON.

Not wanting it smashed.

DANIEL.

Meaning your head.

SAMSON.

No, meaning your 'cello.   But I shall proceed with
her.   She is unhappy—I think she needs *me* !

Enter MORDECAI, *with a piece of lace, by way of the
bridge.   He goes into the shop.*

I thought we had done with trade in this street.
There goes an old sheep to pawn his fleece.   I say
—bah !

DANIEL.

So will the old sheep say " Bah ! " when Sachel has
shorn him.   See the old man feeling it over—they
say he can tell brass from gold by the touch of his
talons.

SAMSON.

It is well the old man is blind ; if he saw the look of
disgust on the girl's face—ay, she'd like to rush out in
the air !

DANIEL.

If she hates trade so, why does she stay in the Ghetto?

SAMSON.

She has nowhere else to go—she doesn't appear to want to get away. Are they cursing each other over a copper? See the curl of her lip! Look! look!

[ROSA *rushes out of the shop*.

ROSA.

[*As if stifling*.] Oh! oh! they have no souls—there is not a soul among them, save Rafael's!

[*She sees* DANIEL *and* SAMSON.

SAMSON.

Good evening!

ROSA.

[*Coldly*.] Good evening.

SAMSON.

It's a fine evening, isn't it?

ROSA.

No.

SAMSON.

No, I suppose not. Is Rafael at home?

ROSA.

No.

SAMSON.

No—he stays away, he is in love?

DANIEL.

With whom?

SAMSON.

With somebody—somebody. I read between the notes of his music. He's fallen in love and he's put it all into music. [*Insinuatingly.*] Do you know who she is?

ROSA.

[*She gets a broom and begins to sweep.*] How should I, a Christian, be so deep in his confidence?

SAMSON.

As deep in his confidence as need be. But do not trust him too much. Ah—[*quasi-regretful*]—and I am his friend. But it is love that has made a fool of me.

ROSA.

No, I should not lay it to the door of love.

SAMSON.

It *is* love. If I could look into such eyes as yours,

and my heart not smoke like—like a burning hay-
cock, then I should be more fool than now.

ROSA.

You could not be. With whom do you mean to
insinuate that Rafael is carrying on a love affair?

SAMSON.

Oh, not you!

ROSA.

Oh! With whom, then?

SAMSON.

[*Whispering.*] To-morrow, when you are alone——
                    [*He pauses, hearing* SACHEL *in the shop.*

SACHEL.

No, no!

MORDECAI.

But——

SACHEL.

No, no, no!

          Enter MORDECAI, *followed by* SACHEL.

MORDECAI.

Half a guilder! Half a guilder! Oh! if it isn't
worth four guilders, it is worth nothing.
                    [*He begins to roll up his lace.*

SACHEL.

If it is worth four guilders to you, keep it.   H'm !
Because I am blind, cannot I feel with my fingers ?
No, it is tatters.

MORDECAI.

It's beautiful.   I leave it to any one.

SACHEL.

So do I.   I leave it to Rosa; she's a Christian, she
knows nothing about trade.   Rosa !

ROSA.

[*Coming to him.*] Yes.

SACHEL.

Am I not right ?   Is it not charity to offer him
half a guilder for that lace ?

DANIEL.

[*Mischievously.*] A beautiful piece of lace !

SAMSON.

A splendid piece of lace; he could not have come
honestly by that !

SACHEL.

I have not summoned every idler in the street.
Rosa!   [*Exeunt* DANIEL *and* SAMSON.

MORDECAI.

[*Whispering to* ROSA.] My son is dead, how can I
bury him without money ? It was his mother's—the
only fragment I have left of hers——

SACHEL.

I hear you ; is he giving you something ?

ROSA.

[*In compassion.*] It is not so badly worn; surely it is
worth four guilders !

SACHEL.

You lie ! I say you lie ! Do you think you can make
a fool of me—you thieves! Ah, I know you are
standing there, twisting your cheeks at me ! But you
shall not rob me ; no, no ! Give me that ! [*He takes
the lace and examines it with his fingers.*] I know it !
It has been patched—by some bag-maker. You minx
—you hussy ! Do I feed you that you may rob me ?
Everybody lies to me—but they do not deceive me !
I will not give half a guilder—only thirty cents.

MORDECAI.

Sachel! I must have *two* guilders! He died in my arms. You have a son—for pity's sake—for pity's sake!

SACHEL.

Have you had pity on my eyes? You say this lace is whole; it is a lie. You say your son is dead; that is a lie too, for all I know. I'll give no more—no more.

MORDECAI.

Oh! Oh! Give me that! You black-hearted miser. [*He snatches it.*] You are rich—you have known me for years—and you would let my son be buried in the pauper's field! A curse on you! May your son *live* to hate you—desert you—disown you—curse you, as I do! [*Exit* MORDECAI.

SACHEL.

Rosa! Run and offer him a guilder and a half! Run!

ROSA.

Mordecai! He will not stop! He's gone!

SACHEL.

With a curse! Could I be more cursed than I am? Come here. You have driven the trade from my door.

ROSA.

I ?

SACHEL.

Yes, you—you misbegotten wretch! Had you not whined and pleaded for him, he would have taken a guilder. If you, too, had said, "Tatters! nothing but tatters." Why did you not?

ROSA.

Because I will not lie for you!

SACHEL.

I employ you to do my bidding! What are you doing now—idling, wasting precious time? [ROSA *begins to sweep.*] In the middle of last night—were you up?

ROSA.

No!

SACHEL.

[*Ironically.*] You will not lie for me! Why are you so disturbed about it?

ROSA.

I am not disturbed.

SACHEL.

I say you are. You are red in the face—I know it. Why were you up?

Rosa.

I was not up.

Sachel.

I heard you! I heard you, and you cannot deceive me. Did I not lie awake until Rafael came home? It struck twelve as he went to his room. It was not five minutes later when I hear steps along the hall —yes, I can hear steps, though the shoes be off! I heard steps, and then your door opened. Why do you stop? I heard your door open; what does it mean?

Rosa.

Do you mean that—that some one came—some one opened my door?

Sachel.

Some one—some one! I mean you—you opened it —and you went downstairs. Why? What were you doing while you thought I slept?

Rosa.

I did not leave my room.

Sachel.

And she will not lie for me! If you are honest, does your voice tremble so? You were up, and why ?   If I miss anything ;—do you want to be turned into the streets? [*He hears the noise of a window opening.*]   Who's that ?   Some fresh enemy ?   I cannot move but some one's hand is raised against me ! Enemies—enemies I cannot strike nor battle with—because I cannot see !

ROSA.

I—I am not your enemy !

SACHEL.

How do I know ?   Have I ever looked into your eyes ?   Ay, if I could look into them at this moment, God knows what I should find.   You are not my enemy !   Why, then, were you up last night prowling about my house—at midnight—when my son—when Rafael ;—Rafael— ?   Come here !   [*She comes to him.*] Your hand !   Was it Rafael ?   Did Rafael— ?   No, no, my beautiful boy—with such as you—an ugly, misshapen wench like you !   [*Pause.*]   Unless— unless they lied to me !   Did not Esther sniff and say that you were white and thin, when we rescued you from pauperdom—when you were threatened with the streets—you thankless vagabond?   They knew I would not have had you else !   Rafael said that "pretty" was no word for such a face as yours ; did he mean

that you were beautiful ;—did he mean that ? Your
form—yes, your form ! [*He passes his hand over her.*]
Hold still ! Do you fear an old blind wreck like me ?
Ay, you are like a Madonna, damn you ! Your face
—hold still—your nose—[*he passes his hand over her
face*]—your brow—your chin ;—they lied to me ! You
are beautiful ! It *was* Rafael !

ROSA.

What do you mean ? I tell you I am not beautiful !

SACHEL.

Are you ugly ? Do you swear you are ugly ?

ROSA.

You cannot see the colour of my skin—you cannot
see the rings under my eyes.

SACHEL.

You swear—do you swear you are not beautiful ?

ROSA.

I may have been pretty once—but now——

[*She is silent.*

SACHEL.

[*Thoughtfully.*] When she says that—h'm ! H'm !

No woman would deny her beauty if she had it. No, no! H'm! Rafael—my beautiful boy; why, I only mentioned it to frighten you!

Enter ESTHER, *over the bridge.*

ESTHER.

What's the matter now—you troublesome old person?

SACHEL.

My sister—my compassionate sister! H'm! I know you're waiting, watching my face from day to day for a sign of death.

ESTHER.

You silly old man, does any one put a pin in your way?

SACHEL.

Any one? Every one! Has she not just driven away a customer because she would not——

ESTHER.

I don't want to hear about it!

SACHEL.

H'm! A little money—it is nothing! I have given my life for it—and my eyes—my eyes! By

God's right, do not the blessings of thrift belong to
me ?   And here I drag my gloomy, empty life away,
with a son who brings me nothing, a sister who
watches me like a vulture and this hussy who drives
my customers to curse me !

ESTHER

Who do you think gave me this letter for you ?
Aaron.

SACHEL.

Aaron !   He hasn't been near us for years !   What
does he want ?   Read !

ESTHER.

When the Sabbath has already begun ?

SACHEL.

Well, what do we have this Christian for ?   Rosa !

Enter ROSA.

ESTHER.

Rosa, open this letter and read it.

ROSA.

[*Reading.*] " I shall be at your house to-night, on a
matter of business.—AARON HEINE."   [*Exit* ROSA.

SACHEL.

Business ?   What business can he have with me ?

ESTHER.

His daughter, I think.   There was something in
the way he spoke that made me feel it !

SACHEL.

To marry his Rebecca to my son.   H'm !   I'll
make him speak first.   I'll worry him !   I'll make
him sweat

ESTHER.

Rosa !   Put up the shutters.

SACHEL.

I will not trust her to put up the shutters.

ESTHER.

You never had a better servant in your house.

SACHEL.

[*Fetches shutters and awkwardly adjusts them.*]
She is a Christian.   It is bad luck—it was wrong for
us to take her in.

ESTHER.

You were glad enough to have her.   Would a

Jewess light your fire on Sabbath—would a Jewess open your letters for you? Shall I send her away?

SACHEL.

Not yet.

ESTHER.

No. Because on Sabbath your feet would be cold and your letters would lie unopened, even if you were not blind. I pity the girl; I have heard that her father was a gentleman and died poor and in exile, because he had given succour to the persecuted Jews.

Enter ROSA.

SACHEL.

Who can prove it? It is a good story to work upon our sympathies. They cannot deceive me. I will have no sympathies.

ESTHER.

[*To* ROSA.] Isn't it warm.

[*They look off over the river.*

ROSA.

But aren't those clouds beautiful? They are bringing a blessed rain; but they lower as if they brought a pestilence.

B

ESTHER.

You call them beautiful?   You know very well
that we are speculating in produce : if the drought
keeps on the rich will have to pay dear for their
vegetables, and the poor won't have any ; it will
profit us handsomely!   And you only think of your
own pleasure !

ROSA.

It was only the beauty, the majesty of the clouds ;
they are massed together like enemies ready to
destroy us.   But the poor ; ah, I can see the hand of
God in those clouds !

ESTHER.

Which God, Rosa ?

ROSA.

The God of all peoples, of all faiths—the God who
knows no ceremony but the way of living, and no
creed but what He plants in the hearts of every one.

ESTHER.

You are a strange sort of Christian!   You talk
like Rafael!   [*Exit* ROSA, *as if to avoid the subject.*]
I wonder if she ever talks with Rafael!   Sachel, I
see Aaron !

SACHEL.

I'll make him speak first.

Enter AARON.

AARON.

[*To* SACHEL.] Good evening. [*No answer.*] What's the matter with you, old friend? I have a bit of business with you.

ESTHER.

Good evening. Rather late for business, isn't it Sit down.

AARON.

It's never too late for business. It was never too early when we were young—eh, Sachel? Do you remember forty years ago, when you and I and Abram stood in line at two o'clock in the morning—to get the best places at the sale? Poverty wasn't trumps then, as it is now.

ESTHER.

H'm! I fancy not with you, now.

SACHEL.

What did you come about?

AARON.

Eh? Well, I have something I think you'll want.

SACHEL.

What ?

AARON.

Eh? Why, some wool. I'll sell it cheap. Feel that! As soft as my daughter's cheek!

> [*Gives* SACHEL *a packet of wool.*

SACHEL.

[*Returning the packet.*] I didn't think you'd have anything I wanted.

ESTHER.

No; it wouldn't interest us. Have some coffee, Rosa!

AARON.

You think it is not good. You don't know! That wool was bought by my daughter, Rebecca, and I'll back her judgment against any man's in the Ghetto! [*Gives a little to* SACHEL.] Feel that!

SACHEL.

[*Breaking the fibres, and listening to the sound they make.*] His daughter! Cotton! More cotton! His daughter!

AARON.

I will match her with your son, any day!

SACHEL.

My son is in no hurry to marry.

AARON.

Marry? I meant as a judge of wool. You are the only one that's thinking of marrying him. What's the matter—doesn't any girl's father want him?

SACHEL.

[*Picking the wool apart.*] H'm!

AARON.

There *is* a keen demand for handsome young wives nowadays, judging from the way my daughter is besieged.

SACHEL.

Your daughter? You speak as if she had had an offer.

Enter ROSA *with the coffee.*

AARON.

H'm, *an* offer! But I came here to talk about wool! If it were not the Sabbath I would burn a little for you, and you could tell by the smell there is not a shred of cotton in it!

SACHEL.

Let the Christian burn it for us, then. Rosa, light that!

[Rosa *burns a little of the wool in the spirit lamp.*

AARON.

[*Laughingly.*] If you can smell cotton in that, then the sheep have been eating cotton-seed, and it has sprouted through their skins. Do you smell any cotton? Ah! [*Exit* Rosa.

SACHEL.

No; because I have picked all the cotton out. Rubbish!

ESTHER.

Have some coffee?

AARON.

[*Putting away packet of wool.*] Oh, well, if you don't know a good thing when you see it. Ah! Those cakes of yours, Esther; I remember them, I remember them of old! Let me send my daughter to learn how to make them, will you?

ESTHER.

Certainly.

AARON.

That's the only thing under the sky that my

daughter can't do to perfection. Well, how is that son of yours?

SACHEL.

Where is he, you had better ask! Unless I stay up till midnight, I never meet him.

AARON.

Oh, well, a young fellow has to have his day I suppose.

SACHEL.

Did I have my day? I was one of eight souls who crawled and starved in a room half as big as my shop parlour. I have known hunger to gnaw at my belly, till I cried myself to sleep, and dreamt that I was disembowelled. And my grandmother died, and my little sister too, from sheer want. Sheer want! At his age I could have bought and sold him twice a day. The fellow is a worthless vagabond!

AARON.

H'm. I suppose, if the truth be said, he *is* a worthless vagabond!

SACHEL.

You—what affair is it of yours? You would give half you have—and that wouldn't be much—to have him in your household!

AARON.

Ha! My daughter has no haste to wed.

SACHEL.

Who said anything about wedding? It is you that seem to have the subject on your mind.

AARON.

With my girl? With Rebecca? You rely too much upon your son's good looks and upon the lot of money he will have.

SACHEL.

Who said he would have a lot of money? I am not dead yet.

AARON.

Even so, your only child is not going empty-handed.

SACHEL.

He will go empty-handed, by the Commandments, if he does not obey his father! And, in any case, I have not slaved my eyes away that another man's child may be fed.

Enter REBECCA.

AARON.

Still he must marry some day.

SACHEL.

Marry whom ? No girl who does not bring twelve thousand guilders shall marry my son ! [*Exit* ESTHER.
[REBECCA *pauses at the bridge unobserved and interested.*

REBECCA.

[*Aside.*] They are getting on !

AARON.

[*Swelling with indignation.*] Twelve thousand guilders ! Twelve thousand guilders ! A snap of the finger ! And is your son a prince ? You talk like an imbecile. Suppose some one was fool enough to give his daughter such a dowry, what would you give your son ?

SACHEL.

Nothing ! He has his share in the business—or will have.

AARON.

Oh, you're enough to make a man jump into the sea !

SACHEL.

Did I ask anything of you ? Why should you jump into the sea ?

AARON.

Eh, what? Rebecca! How did *you* happen to be here?

SACHEL.

[*Ironically.*] Yes, how did you happen to be here?

REBECCA.

Why, didn't you *tell* me——

AARON.

[*Waving her away.*] We're talking business, Sachel and I!

Enter ESTHER.

Esther, those cakes are wonderful!

ESTHER.

Thanks! [*To* REBECCA.] Look here. [*Showing a photograph—watching her closely.*] Rafael is a good-looking boy, isn't he?

REBECCA.

Oh, you'd better let me have this! He wouldn't mind, would he? What a fine likeness—but so sad!

ESTHER.

That's for some nice girl to take out of him.

REBECCA.

[*Tapping the photograph.*] And you'll let me——

ESTHER.

Have the picture ?   With pleasure !   Have you seen Isaac's new warehouse ?

> [*Points up the canal.*   REBECCA *retires to the bridge.*

[*Sotto, to* AARON.] I like your girl—she's remarkably discreet.   When she's married, you'll be lonely enough !

AARON.

[*Sotto.*] And when she is married, Esther—[*meaningly*]—may I take me a wife on the same day ; one that can bake such cakes as those ! [*Aloud.*] Esther, there is not another woman in Amsterdam that can bake such cakes as those !

> [*The two exchange meaning glances ; they advance on* SACHEL, *as if now in alliance.*

REBECCA.

[*Aside.*] I don't believe it was about me !

AARON.

But, outside of that, Rebecca is a wonderful house-wife, and in the shop—she brings me the trade !

SACHEL.

H'm! She'll never bring you a son-in-law! For you can't spare money to give with her. You need it all in your business.

AARON.

Do I? With my daughter there will go a trifle of eight thousand guilders.   [*Pause.*

REBECCA.

[*Aside.*] It *is* about me.   They are getting on !

AARON.

And he thinks a girl will bring his son a matter of twelve thousand guilders.

Enter ROSA ; *she shows that she has been listening and is troubled.*

SACHEL.

Let my son tell me he is going to marry a girl with less than twelve thousand ! I would give him the choice of starvation.   I would lock the door on him.

[ROSA *sees the photograph in* REBECCA'S *hand.*

AARON.

Who's talking of your son ? My daughter—Esther, ust look at her—such a figure, such a skin—such

eyes! Esther, Esther, look at her walk! Look at
her walk!

REBECCA.

Is Rafael at home?

ROSA.

No.

ESTHER.

Rafael and Rebecca—that would sound rather well!

AARON.

My dear woman, I won't give twelve thousand
guilders.

SACHEL.

And I won't give my son at less!

AARON.

Your son? Did I ask you for your son? Did I?

SACHEL.

Did I ask you for your daughter? What is she to
me?

REBECCA.

[*Aside.*] Oh, they are really getting on!

AARON.

Oh, my daughter! I wish your son were her equal!
If *I* had such a son——

SACHEL.

I don't want your advice! [*Rises.*] You manag
your own child.   I'll manage mine.   [*Starts for shop.*

AARON.

You will?   You can't manage him.   Where is he
now?   Dallying with some wanton, for all you know!
My God, one would think him a second Joseph!

SACHEL.

Do you house him?   Do you feed him?   Does he
trouble you?   Speak well of him, or go home!

AARON.

I will go home!

ESTHER.

Sit down!   Now talk sense!   It's a good match:
you both know it's a good match, and so—[*to* REBECCA]
—have you seen the repairs to the old bridge?

> [REBECCA *moves farther away, leaving the photo-
> graph of* RAFAEL *on the wall.*

[*Lowering her voice.*] They are both only children.
And so, in any case, the money will stay in the family.
You let Sachel consider it.

> [ROSA *takes the photograph of* RAFAEL *and hides
> it behind her.*

REBECCA.

[*Aside.*] I wonder how Rafael will consider it?

SACHEL.

It costs nothing to consider it, but——

ESTHER.

We'll see you to-morrow.

AARON.

At my house—before service.   Come on, Rebecca;
I have arranged about the wool.   Good-night!

[*Exit.*

ESTHER.

Good-night!

REBECCA.

Oh, where's my picture of Rafael? [ROSA *drops the
photograph into the canal.*] It's gone!

[*She looks about for it.*

ESTHER.

How could it have gone?

[REBECCA *sees it in the canal.*

REBECCA.

It has fallen into the canal!   It's ruined!   [*Looks
at* ROSA.] I don't understand.   I don't understand!

ESTHER.

Oh, well; Rafael has some others. I'll see Rafael. Good-night.

REBECCA.

[*To* ROSA.] If the portrait dropped in where I left it, then it must have floated against the current.

ROSA.

[*Fiercely, sotto.*] It did go against the current.

[*Exit* REBECCA.

SACHEL.

Not a cent under twelve thousand.

[ROSA, *at the bridge, struggles with tears.*

ESTHER.

We shall see!   [*Exit.*

SACHEL.

So we shall. Why doesn't he come? His miserable selfishness. My God, if anything has happened to him! He doesn't come. He might have been set upon and robbed—beaten, killed, by some cursed ruffian beyond the Ghetto. My God—I'm harsh —too harsh with him. I shall be chastened for it. I was harsh to his mother; yes, I know—I know; I broke her heart perhaps, and Rafael, poor boy—— [*Stops, listens.*] His step! Yes; even—steady—he's in no distress. He's not worrying about *me*. He'll come home to sleep and get more money—that's all. He's a vagabond—a rascally vagabond!

Enter Esther.

Enter Rafael *by the bridge.*

RAFAEL.

[*Wearily.*] Good evening. [*No answer.*] Good evening! [*No answer.*]

[*He exchanges guarded looks with* Rosa. *Exit* Rosa.

ESTHER.

[*Contemptuously.*] The gentleman says "Good evening!" This is his lodging-house, where he does us the honour to sleep!

RAFAEL.

I know I am rather late. I hope you were not anxious about me, father. Were you? Father! Oh—well!

ESTHER.

Why should he answer you? What manner of son are you?

SACHEL.

Where have you been all day?

RAFAEL.

I—what does it matter? I know—I promised to do some business for you—but—there were other things— I forgot—I am sorry.

ESTHER.

Oh, he's sorry.

SACHEL.

I asked you where you idled all this day, and you evaded me.

RAFAEL.

I have been everywhere—and the day vanished while I was thinking. Have you something to eat, aunt?

SACHEL.

We have finished eating.

ESTHER.

At this time of night! Il'm!

RAFAEL.

Very well. I will see what I can find.

SACHEL.

Oh, my Maker, how heavily thou visitest upon me! To be thus mocked by a stranger within mine own house! If your poor dead mother knew how you treated me!

RAFAEL.

Father, the rotten board that marked my mother's grave is falling to pieces. And you can hardly find the spot for weeds—weeds!

SACHEL.

Is that where you've been? Where else?

RAFAEL.

Far away—in my thoughts.

SACHEL.

Another day—a whole precious day devoured by your drivelling nonsense! Are you a son? Have you an old blind father? Oh, my business, my splendid business, that I slaved and sweated out my marrow for, dwindling, dwindling with every ticking of the clock! And he wants me to buy a new head-board! I had better buy one for myself. I had better be dead than not, with such a son.

ESTHER.

Sachel! Sachel! You cry—for a son like that! He is not worth one tear.

SACHEL.

God punishes me for all my sins. When he was a child I have stolen the bread from my mouth for him, weeks at a time; and now I may burrow alone in the dark for all he cares, chained to my door-post, chained to wait till some one comes to deal with me—to rob and swindle and mock me—because I am alone—and blind.

RAFAEL.

And the saddest is, it is not my doing, and I cannot help it.

SACHEL.

Not his doing! Oh, my Maker! Can I keep him in irons and make him use his eyes for me?

RAFAEL.

Father, between us matters cannot be improved—now nor ever!

ESTHER.

Well, upon my word!

SACHEL.

Why not? You have something you dare not tell. There is a woman in it. You had forty guilders when you went away this morning. Have you a cent of it left?

RAFAEL.

I gave it all to Mordecai to bury his son.

SACHEL.

I do not believe it.

RAFAEL.

Father! For the little time that I remain here need we add more bitterness to what exists?

SACHEL.

What do you say?

RAFAEL.

I am going away.

SACHEL.

What—what—what do you say?

RAFAEL.

I am going away!

SACHEL.

Oh, oh, that crowns all! He can look into my dead eyes and threaten this—without a quiver—without a qualm!

RAFAEL.

Ah, there was a time—there was a time, when I would have yielded any sacrifice for you—when I was a boy and you had just gone blind, and my heart was wrung with a pity for you that was a very pity in itself. If I had seen tears in your poor sightless eyes, then my peace would have been utterly destroyed; at the thought of having vexed you I should have beaten my brow. And now it's gone—gone—and it won't come back—it can't come back—because you robbed me of it.

SACHEL.

I? I? What have *I* done? And why do you go away?

RAFAEL.

For reasons all of which I will not tell.

SACHEL.

You dog! To leave your father—sick and blind, and on the road to poverty! God shall curse you for it!

RAFAEL.

No; God shall not! To live under this roof—to see, day in, day out—nothing—nothing—but, no—no! There *are* reasons, reasons enough, Heaven be my judge!

> [*Several musical instruments begin to tune up in the house where* DANIEL *and* SAMSON *live.*

Esther.

Heaven will be your judge! There *are* reasons—
reasons you are ashamed of—reasons you dare not
tell!

Sachel.

It is true! You have fouled my name, you have
been in the mire, you have committed some con-
temptible thing you are ashamed of! You are
running away, you dare not tell why!

[Rafael *throws over a chair; regains his com-
posure.*

Rafael.

Is it but three years ago that I was so ignorant, so
raw, and so fond of you? I had known you with
the fire of life in your eyes, and now it had gone; the
light of your soul was as hidden in a dungeon, because you were blind. Ah, how I suffered! I shut
my eyes to imagine it—darkness, black nothing; God's
beautiful sky gone for ever, as if you were in your
coffin under ground! Awful! Awful! And this,
this was my father—my father, whom I loved and
honoured, of all the world!

Sachel.

Who asked your sympathy? Hold your tongue!

Rafael

I honoured you because you asked the sympathy of no man. I *honoured* you. Shall I ever forget that Friday, when I stood alone in the gloom of this warehouse, watching you, sorrowing over your blindness, with tears in my eyes! You stood by the scales. They were weighing out your merchandise; the man who had bought it stooped and shifted the weights; and your creature Jacob read the figures out and you wrote them down in great coarse scrawls—your grey head bare, your face turned up to heaven. How I loved you—how I pitied you! You bore yourself with such calm—such fortitude—as if, when God had touched your eyes, He had whispered into your ears some portion of the everlasting truth. No one saw me—I was back in the shadow. And I started forward; I wanted to say, "Father—go in; father, never labour again! Sit in your chair—rest always—while I do your bidding—while I do everything!" But I did not say it. No! I stopped; I slunk back into the deepest shadow like a criminal. I had uttered a cry, but you and Jacob did not hear me. On the platform of the scales, when your client stooped to balance them, I had seen a foot go out—go out while your white face was turned in holy calm to heaven—

go out and press down—so that the scales read false—
so that the man who bought our goods was tricked
and robbed—robbed of the money we had not earned
from him.   And again I saw it, and again, and again,
father!   And the man whose foot went out and did
this crime, the man who was stealing and stealing,
time after time, stealing his money, stealing my
respect, my honour, my youth, before my eyes—was
it Jacob?   No, it was you—you, my father—my
father, whom I loved and pitied, and they had trusted
—because you were blind !

ESTHER.

Shame !   That's a lie !   Shame !

RAFAEL.

[*Turning to his father.*] Is it a lie ?

SACHEL.

[*Hoarsely.*] Let him go on.   Let him go on.

RAFAEL.

And that afternoon I went with my father to the
synagogue; I did not pray, I could not speak.   I
only gazed at my father's face, waiting to see it soften
into some shade of doubt, of repentance, of remorse.
And the dead eyes faced up to the rafters where the

sun shone through—they faced up there with the same impassive stare—the same holy calm, as when he stood with his foot on the scales. Ah, when we walked home, how cold and pitiless the sky looked down at me that winter day! We sat at our Sabbath table. He complained that I was silent. He said prayers, he dipped the bread in the salt. The lamplight shone on him, and I stared into his face, and I saw nothing—nothing I had always thought I saw—and my heart was ice; and he rose and stumbled over a stool and fell, and I picked him up—and my heart was still ice. He was no longer blind to me—he was nothing—nothing but a—ah no, no,—what's the use —what's the use?

SACHEL.

[*Hoarsely.*] Have I been different from the others? Aaron, Levy, Isaac, would they not have done the same? Is there any one who would not take advantage of my eyes? No; business is business.

RAFAEL.

Business,—Aaron, Levy, Isaac! God, how I have despised them all my life!

ESTHER.

Oh, he would give overweight!

RAFAEL.

I will quarrel no more with you. When I am gone——

SACHEL.

You are not going—you shall not go ! [*Trembling.*] I have nothing in the world but you. Didn't I do it all for you? When I am dead the money will be yours, and the blame sewed up in my shroud with me. Can't you be content ?

RAFAEL.

[*After looking at him for a moment, hopelessly.*] It is getting late. I am tired. Let us go to bed, and to-morrow let us part friends.

ESTHER.

You eat something. Then you'll feel differently. H'm ! He go away ! I shall call up Rosa !

RAFAEL.

Thanks, no. I could not eat now. Has she not done enough this sweltering day ?

ESTHER.

Then I'm going to bed. No wonder, to be so

irregular in your ways. You were up last night.
Couldn't you sleep ?

RAFAEL.

I did not sleep until nearly morning.

[*Exit* ESTHER. SACHEL *goes to try the shutters.*
Well, good-night, father. You won't answer ?
Well, good-night ! [*Music begins in the house at the
back.*] [*Aside.*] They are playing my music. Give
me time—I will show you what is in my soul !

SACHEL.

[*Aside.*] The scales—that is not the only reason !

Enter ROSA, *who does not see* SACHEL. *She starts to go
to* RAFAEL. SACHEL *hears her.*

Rosa, why are you not in bed ? [ROSA *stops motion-
less, mute, frightened.*] Is that Rosa ? [*He is suspicious.*
[*They do not answer. Exit* SACHEL *into the
house, evidently with a purpose.*

ROSA.

[*Rushing to* RAFAEL.] Rafael ! Rafael ! Tell me
the truth. Am I not your wife ? Don't you love me ?
Do you love some one else ? Do you love Aaron's
daughter ? They are planning to marry her to you.

What does it mean? [*He motions her to be silent.*]
Does it mean that you wish it? No—no, it can't be
that: you have said you were going away; but you
didn't tell them of me. Why? Why do you not
tell them of me?—soon enough you'll have to; and
then—then you will have to choose—choose between
the rage of your father—between disinheritance—
poverty—the wrath of all the Ghetto, and me—only
me! Rafael, my life is in your hands. Love me—love
me, Rafael! Don't let me doubt you! [*He stops her
mouth. Suddenly* SACHEL *opens the window over the
shop-door; he leans out, listens, hears nothing, withdraws.*]
He's in my room—he's searching for me—he suspects
us—he has said so. He's coming down now; he's
going to accuse us; he's going to tell you to desert
me—desert me or starve! Rafael, what are you going
to say? Rafael, what are you going to say?

[*He stops her mouth again; they look in through
the door. A pause.*

Enter SACHEL.

SACHEL.

She's not in the house! Rosa—where are you?

ROSA.

[*Whispering to* RAFAEL.] Where? Where?

RAFAEL.

[*Quietly taking her in his arms.*] Rosa is here, father.

A WATCHMAN.

[*Heard in the distance.*] Ten o'clock, and all's well ! Ten o'clock, and all's well !

[SACHEL *shakes his head.*

END OF THE FIRST ACT.

THE SECOND ACT

Scene : *A living room in the rear of* Sachel's *shop. A door at the back opens into the street ; at the left a staircase runs up over a fireplace to a gallery which gives access to two rooms off the stage.*

Rosa *is discovered at the fireplace.* Esther *is at the dining-table, which is set with the Sabbath-cloth.* Esther *crosses to a door at the left.*

Esther.

Sachel, your medicine !

[Rosa *brings a jug of hot water to the table ;* Esther *prepares some medicine with the water.*

Enter Sachel.

Sachel.

That girl—where is she ?

ESTHER.

She's here.

SACHEL.

[*Aside.*] That's what Rafael said last night. Rosa! Go and water the flowers in my window and pick off the dead leaves, and be sure you give plenty of time to it.   [*Exit* ROSA.

ESTHER.

Well! Since when have you taken such an interest in flowers?   [*She goes upstairs.*

SACHEL.

I want to talk; I've been awake all night. This girl keeps lying to me. Last night she had the effrontery to tell me—[*with calculation*]—she told me she was considered beautiful!

ESTHER.

[*Not interested.*] Well, she is beautiful!
                    [*Exit* ESTHER.

SACHEL.

H'm! [*He thinks deeply ; rises.*] Ròsa!

Enter ROSA.

Last night you tried to make me think you were ugly;

—you deceived me. You are not a woman—you are a fiend come into my house—come in out of the Christian world—to do what? What do you expect to do here? Do you know you are in the heart of the Ghetto? What do you expect to do in my house?

Rosa.

Nothing but what my God gives me the right to do!

Sachel.

Your God? I tell you the wall your God built against us still shuts Him away from here! You came into my house to divide it against itself. You have been getting too near my son. Do you think I don't know? You've been trying to turn him against his religion, you've been trying to turn him against me!

Rosa.

If I have, then I have failed. Rafael loves you.

Sachel.

You say so? I ask no better proof that he hates me! You came into my house to accomplish this, you vampire! Could you not have fastened on some-

D

one else than Rafael? Who sent you here to find
him? Did your Christian God send you here?

ROSA.

[*Thinking of* RAFAEL.] Yes, yes, my God did send me
here—[*checks herself*]—or else I should have starved.

SACHEL.

Starve! Does a demon ever starve? Not while
young men have hot blood! Hah! It is well that I
have found you out before this thing has gone too
far. Don't I know your damned tricks; *you* wouldn't
be satisfied with a passing touch of his lips. You've
got a brain—a lying, scheming, devilish brain! You
want his heart—you want his soul! By God! [*He
goes vigorously and opens the door, to the street.*] Do
you know what I'm going to do? There's where
we found you—out there in the streets, without a
friend, without a cent, and your dead father——

ROSA.

Sachel, my father helped your people!

SACHEL.

Now let the Jews help his daughter! You've
lied to me always! Shall I believe this story of your

father? I believe he was a demon like you! I believe he was sent out of hell to steal away men's souls, as you were. You've found something to fight when you've come across me! Shall I feel a snake in my bosom and not cast it out? [*He points to the door.* You— [*He checks himself; a pause.*] Shut the door! Go on with your work! [*Exit* Rosa.] No, no, no —it won't do to *tear* him away from her. She is beautiful;—we must marry him to Rebecca. Rebecca is handsome, Rebecca is rich, Rebecca is minx enough. We must marry him to Rebecca if we can. If not, to some one else—any one else, as soon as we can. But we must handle him with care. Ah! I had better get the Rabbi to talk to him; the Rabbi has tact. And, for the present, we must let Rosa be.

Enter Esther.   *A knock on the door.*

Aaron.   Come in!

Enter Aaron.

AARON.

Good morning!

SACHEL.

Good morning!

ESTHER.

Good morning!

AARON.

I shouldn't have come, my friend, if I hadn't promised Esther. For I've been thinking it over; and if there is any question of your son marrying my daughter, I tell you I will give eight thousand guilders and no more!

SACHEL.

All because I said " Good morning " to you. I have been considering it. I am willing to talk with you. As you probably said in your sleep last night, if you can get rid of your daughter without paying more than ten thousand guilders, you'll be pretty well satisfied.

AARON.

Eh—what ?

SACHEL.

Come on, it's time to start to the synagogue; we'll have a talk on the way.

AARON.

But, my dear sir, eight thousand——

SACHEL.

No ; as you said in your sleep—ten thousand !

[*Exeunt all.*

Enter SAMSON, *cautiously.*

SAMSON.

Rosa! Rosa! [*Aside.*] A little show of modesty!
Rosa! Nevertheless she is listening at the other
side of that door; she thinks I will betray myself in
some soliloquy. H'm! [*Loudly.*] Ah—she's not
here; how the blood rushed to my heart, like the
sea beating against a rock, when I thought I should
have two golden moments alone with her! [*He stands
on lowest cupboard shelf to be near her door, which is
upstairs.*] But she's gone!—gone forth to air her
beauty. Such beauty! Such a face, such a form!
Night after night she floats in my dreams—[*he
steps up one shelf nearer*]—for I love her so that I
have not slept a wink for weeks.

Enter DANIEL, *unobserved by* SAMSON.

And if she were here I would tell her so! I could
gratify her tastes! For once her love is mine. [*He
draws a bunch of keys from his pocket.*] She shall hear
such music as this from morn till night——

[*He jingles the keys.*

Enter ROSA.

One—two—three—four—five—five gold pieces! Did
I come abroad with only five? H'm! There are
plenty more like these indoors—yes, in doors! And

here I stand perishing with my ardour. Nay, I feel
faint—— [DANIEL *bursts into loud laughter.*

ROSA.

[*To* SAMSON.] You miserable cur! [SAMSON *descends
sheepishly.*] If I were of your faith—if I were not a
servitor, without a father, without a brother, you
would not dare! [DANIEL *laughs.*] And you—if
you were a little better than he, you would have
struck him! What do you want here? Go!

DANIEL.

Look here, my girl, you need not be so virtuous
when you talk to us! We live next to you—our
windows overlook yours—eh, Samson?

SAMSON.

Don t you be unpleasant to this lady!

ROSA.

[*To* DANIEL.] What do you mean?

DANIEL.

Lady! What do we mean? What's the difference? Rafael is a friend of ours. We are most liberal
—most charitable, eh, Samson?

ROSA.

Rafael? Why do you speak of Rafael? What do you mean?

SAMSON.

Now you needn't bring Rafael into it, Daniel. I don't want any—any misapprehension with Rafael.

ROSA.

You shall have an understanding with him, you cowards—you vulgar beasts! I shall tell him!

DANIEL.

He'll tell you to hold your tongue. Are you his wife? No; you're a Christian servant in his father's house; we know all about that, and you'd better learn to take a joke.

SAMSON.

It was only a joke, you know—only a joke—(*with a forced laugh.*) [ROSA's *anger increases.*] Now don't you tell Rafael that I was trying to get in his way!

ROSA.

What do you mean? Get in his way? He would flick you over his shoulder into the canal. I shall tell him!

Samson.

Don't—don't bring Rafael into it! Hasn't he enough on his mind already?

Rosa.

Would anything so slight as you increase his burden? You cowards! You both fear him! You *may* fear him!

Enter Rafael.

Rafael.

Hallo! News! news! I've seen Hanakoff—and Hanakoff says — Hanakoff — what's the matter? What is the matter? Which of you was it? Rosa, what did they do?

Rosa.

[*Pointing to* Samson.] Let him speak.

Samson.

Why—why, she can't take a joke—that's all.

Rafael.

Oh, a joke. What was the joke? What was the joke?

Daniel.

Oh, everything is a joke. Don't we live across the

street? Can two people help putting their heads
together once in a while? Well, of course, if you—if
she—if we—why, of course——

RAFAEL.

What did they say?

ROSA

They said—they insinuated that—that——

RAFAEL.

I know what they said. You—I— [*He takes hold of
them both.*] Two people can't help putting their heads
together! If you will meet me in some seclusion, my
two good friends, I'll show you how two heads can be
so put together that two people shall see stars enough
to read their horoscopes. You shall read in those
stars the name of Rosa—Rosa who, God search my
soul, is purer than the snows on the crest of the
Jungfrau. Quite properly—[*as he causes them to bend
low*]—quite properly, they bend in homage, Rosa!
And Daniel here, Daniel whom the starving lions
would not taste—the story never seemed to me so
true as now—he says that what he said he did not
say, and can't remember what it was, and is most
sorry that he said it—and see—[*forces them*]—bends
low. I thank you for your courtesy. And Samson,

he that slew the thousands with the jawbone of an ass — which is his jawbone to this day — he's swallowing those words he spoke, so eagerly that he chokes! Ha, ha! my ardent friends! [*He turns them about ironically.*] And must you go? Ah, well! [*He pushes them towards the door.*] If you insist—if you insist—Good-bye! Good-bye! [*He throws them violently out.*] [*Then to* Rosa.] I have seen Hanakoff; he is going to play my music to-night; and if—Rosa— [Rosa *bursts into tears.*] Rosa!

Rosa.

Go away from me!

Rafael.

But why, Rosa——

Rosa.

Let me be! You shall never touch me again! I hate you—I loathe you—all of you!

Rafael.

But have I not disposed of them! Is there anything else? My darling!

Rosa.

No, never again; never shall you lay your hand on me! I know what lies before me now. I am your

wife and you will not proclaim me. I am your wife
and they insult me, and you bundle them off without
a word such as I wanted, as if I were your mistress,
who must not be vexed! I know now; last night
you soothed me over—you took me in your arms
before him; but he is blind—he did not understand—
he only suspected something foul; and so it will grow,
until his suspicion makes an open accusation; and
then you will stand revealed—you will shrink away
from me—you will cry, " I have sinned in the sight
of the synagogue," and I shall be cast out of doors—
a broken plaything, a husk of yesterday!

RAFAEL.

Rosa! Rosa! Are you not my wife?

ROSA.

Your wife—here in the Ghetto—here among your
people? No, to them I am a Christian—to them I
cannot be your wife—to them I am a sacrilege—an
insult in their teeth! Oh! as one who enters hell I
entered here—a steaming hell of avarice; not life—
but a sickly poisoned dream of gain, gain—always
gain. I thought I saw a bright light shining in this
horrid place. I flew to you—I gave you my soul—to
find myself—ugh!—only ——

RAFAEL.

Horror! that you should even think such things!

ROSA.

Think such things! You say you love me with all
your heart—with all your soul. How great is your
soul that dares not the anger of a father who is
wrong?—a soul that fears poverty, disinheritance,
the hatred of the Ghetto? You fear that you would
be cast off, that you would suffer want and ridicule,
that your father would never feed you and clothe you
again; and when that fear comes into your heart
what room is left for me? Love! Ugh! Ugh!
What is *your* love! The love of the way that is
easiest, the love of the son of honest Sachel—the love
of a Jew!

RAFAEL.

[*Slowly, sorrowfully.*] And now *you* say "Jew!"
"Jew!" as they say it in the streets, among the mob,
when I go beyond the Ghetto. It sounds strange
from lips that I thought loved me; it sounds strange
from the daughter of your father! Such a man he
! When you and I had our first long talks
together, and you told me of the noble deeds your
father had done in behalf of the Jews, I couldn't help

loving you for his sake; and now you call me Jew!
I *am* a Jew. Never forget that I am a Jew. I have
married you; and when it is known I shall have no
standing among Jews. The orthodox will avoid me
as a pariah, and the mob of Jews will howl at me
when I go into the street. And I shall still be a Jew
—proud of my race, proud of its fortitude, of the
great triumph which shall come to us Jews when we
have shaken off the material shell which hides our
spirits, and makes us no better and no worse than the
Christians! No, no! You are angry—you don't
care what you say! You are angry—and you sneer
at my father. What do you know against my father's
honesty?

Rosa.

He is the father of a man who has married me and
dares not proclaim me.

Rafael.

Dares not! Dares not! Ah, you little know me
if you think that! Rosa, Rosa! Look here! My
dear little girl, you are all wrong. We have agreed
on this point. It was yourself who said that we must
not tell of our marriage yet. [Rosa *sinks into a chair*.]
You said that I must give my time to my music,
until I had made a name—until we could go forth on

our own footing—not cast out of that door—without
a cent between us, to be reviled and hustled by the
mob. And I thought of my father—of his old age—
of his pain. If he *is* wrong—if he *is* what he should
not be, he's still my father——

Rosa.

He called me a demon just now! He opened the
door and was about to bid me go from here. He said
my father came out of hell. He called me a vampire /
—he called me a snake——

Rafael.

Oh—! Oh—! Rosa, poor little Rosa!

Rosa. .

[*Weeping.*] I only want you to love me. I want
to know it—to know that they cannot, shall not take
you from me! Tell me so, Rafael; burn it into my
heart, Rafael!

Rafael.

Yes, it must be burned into your heart, dear. Before
to-night it shall be. I love you! I dare anything
for the sake of my love for you!

Rosa.

Rafael! [*Knock at the door. She rushes upstairs*

Rafael! But your father—[*knock*]—you mustn't tell him!

RAFAEL.

Hush! [*Exit* ROSA. RAFAEL *goes to the window; sees* REBECCA.] Rebecca! She knows that the old people will be at the synagogue at this hour. What does she want here? A true daughter of her father, and yet she has many virtues, I suppose! I wish she would take her virtues and go home! I want to get at my music.

Enter REBECCA.

Oh, some friend of Rosa, I suppose?

REBECCA.

What—don't you know me? I am Rebecca—I used to know you once.

RAFAEL.

Oh, Rebecca—Abram's daughter, of course. Won't you——? · [*Points to a chair.*

REBECCA.

Not Abram's daughter, Rafael; Aaron's daughter. My father was here only yesterday.

RAFAEL.

Oh, Aaron's daughter! Oh yes! Aaron was here only yesterday!

REBECCA.

Yes.

RAFAEL.

And now you are here.

REBECCA.

Yes. He came to sell some wool.

RAFAEL.

Some wool? I thought it was a lamb he came to sell. Ah well! [*Motions to chair.*] Let us proceed to business.

REBECCA.

But I did not come on business.

RAFAEL.

We are quite alone.

REBECCA.

From what your friends Samson and Daniel have just told me, I should think not.

[*She examines the room.*

RAFAEL.

How do you like it?

REBECCA.

[*Laughs.*] Father said I ought to come and see Esther.

RAFAEL.

Oh, so your father—a thoughtful man; your father, a man of tact, admirable tact!

REBECCA.

You say such strange things!
    [*A pause. She begins to struggle with a ring on her finger.*

RAFAEL.

[*Yawning.*] Admirable tact!

REBECCA.

This ring—it's so tight—it hurts my finger so! I took it from Isaac's son one time—when we played that our fathers had engaged us to marry. I don't suppose it was quite proper of me, was it, Rafael? It was years ago—but—but—[*pulls*]—it doesn't come easily! [*She stretches out her hand to him.*] Don't you want to clear it away, Rafael?

E

RAFAEL.

[*Goes to the cupboard.*] Just a moment.

REBECCA.

[*With her hand still out.*] Everybody out, Rafael?

RAFAEL.

[*Bringing a plate.*] There's not a Jew in the house.
  [*He removes the ring easily, and gives it to her
  on the plate.*

REBECCA.

[*Vexed.*] Your servant—that Christian person—I
suppose she's listening at that door?

RAFAEL.

[*He sits on the table.*] You might go up and see,

REBECCA.

[*After hesitating, she runs up the stairs and opens
the door.*] Oh! I don t believe there is any one in the
house but us! I'm afraid to come down!

RAFAEL.

You needn't be!

REBECCA.

You mustn't come up!

RAFAEL.

They'll be home soon.   Let us proceed to business.

REBECCA.

[*Archly coming down one step.*] Do you call it business ?

RAFAEL.

I can't say I do.   I weigh 12 stone, Rebecca, and your father won't give but 8000 guilders.   That's— that's 666 guilders a stone ; 14 into 666, that's only 45 guilders a pound !   And——

REBECCA.

No, it's over 47½ guilders a pound.

RAFAEL.

I am sure you are right—only 47½ guilders a pound he'll give for me.   No, I can't say I call that business.

REBECCA.

[*Coming down a step.*] You don't seem to have much sentiment about it, Rafael.

RAFAEL.

Ah, if it were only a matter of sentiment ! [*She comes down two steps.*] But sentiment after business;

Rebecca, after business. I am 40 inches round the chest, Rebecca; and if my heart should swell I should be doubtless 45. But at eight thousand guilders, Rebecca, it doesn't swell!

REBECCA.

But I—I don't like to talk this way, Rafael; it doesn't seem to me quite—quite nice.

RAFAEL.

That is your delicacy, Rebecca, your extreme delicacy. But we must not mix delicacy with business, Rebecca. He sticks at eight thousand, and not a thing, I suppose, in the way of dresses, finery, rigging——?

REBECCA.

It's really most unpleasant to have to talk of such things. Of course I shall have a dozen of everything; father has told me so—when I am—when I—I can't say it! I really can't speak of it.

RAFAEL.

That's your shrinking nature, Rebecca, your extreme sensitiveness! H'm! How should a man's heart know which way to beat? On the one side the daughter, with her delicacy, her shrinking nature; on the other side the father, who sticks at eight thousand guilders! No; at eight thousand I will not love you. It would not be dignified at eight thousand!

REBECCA.

[*Coming down the remaining steps.*] But you don't suppose that if my father were willing to give, say, ten thousand, he would begin at more than eight thousand; not with *your* father—now would he, Rafael? But I think that nowadays, when young people are to be—when they intend—they ought to have some sentiment for each other.

RAFAEL.

H'm!

REBECCA.

And, moreover, I think that young men should be more careful as to how they let themselves be talked about—more careful than you are. They call you an infidel, Rafael, and they say disagreeable things about you and this impertinent servant of yours.

RAFAEL.

They do! [*A pause.*] Of course, if we were to contemplate matrimony—you and I—such a matter would be very serious.

REBECCA.

It certainly would.

RAFAEL.

And so it's very fortunate, Rebecca, that we have been talking in a kind of irony—you and I—over a matter which was never even remotely possible! Isn't it?

REBECCA.

[*After a pause.*] Yes, *very* fortunate. It would have been most unfortunate for you if you had ever entertained the idea. If your father or mine entertain it, we must speedily end that. Go on with your scullerymaid; it's nothing to me.

RAFAEL.

No, it's nothing to you, Rebecca! You and I don't want to marry, and they are trying to chain us together against our wills! We must fight them, Rebecca! We must put our backs against the wall! Your father will whisper avarice to you. He'll bid you look around. "This is thy neighbour's house," he'll say. " It will all be Rafael's; see—see—treasure, value, gain; see the jewels there, the gold and silver, the rich laces and old articles of art—all his, my girl —and his father will die soon! He'll die of joy if he gets eight thousand guilders with his daughter-in-law. And then it will be all yours—yours and Rafael's; yours to hug and wrap your soul around, my girl;

all—all, from the last atom of diamond dust in the cases there, to the rust on the nail in the latch on the door that keeps away the moans of the starving!"

REBECCA.

But do you think——?

RAFAEL.

But you won't be betrayed by an old man's lust for gold. No! You'll say: " Father, I have a heart; I will not give myself to one I do not love, to soothe your itching palm!" You'll look well saying that, Rebecca! You'll stand and face him in the dignity of truth! You'll be defending the next generation against the crawling viper of greed! I'd like to be there! I'd like to see the flash in your eyes; even now you cannot think of it without fire in your look! I see the anger of righteousness; I cannot too deeply express my respect, Rebecca!

REBECCA.

Do you think I don't know what you mean? You think I want to marry you—to get you away from this vile creature—this unthinkable person who——

Enter ROSA.

RAFAEL.

Will you be so good as to say no more about Rosa!

If a man— [*He checks himself.*] Let me tell you what she is to me——

Rosa.

Rafael, Rafael !

Rebecca.

Oh ! She calls you Rafael ! She was listening all the time ! What they say is true : you thrust your shameful doings in my face ! I shall tell my father —I shall tell everyone ; they will stone you from the Ghetto ! You tried to make a fool of me ; and you —you—— [*She bursts into tears. Exit.*

Rafael.

And now I'm going to break my poor old father's heart. I am going to tell him that you and I were married by the Civil Authority beyond the Ghetto, that we are one and indivisible. Poor old man ! I am not without love for my father, you know. He will think that I am lost for ever ; he will turn me away from his door with a curse on his lips ; and then, when we are gone, he'll sink down in his chair and weep ; a broken life, an old age come to nothing ! And he may die at any moment—it may kill him— and he *might* have died and never have known it.

Rosa.

Rafael, I can't be the cause of his death ! Don't tell him, Rafael ! I will try to live on—as we are.

Rafael.

Live on as we are, with this doubt in your heart? You have said I dared not face poverty for your sake. Such a doubt must be killed at any cost. I won't have it coming back to you to mar your faith in me in after years. No; there's no question of my not telling him; there's only the question of how to tell him.

Rosa.

Rafael, I would rather you wouldn't ! I have been selfish; I forgot about your father; I forgot about your music.

Rafael.

My father will probably speak first of Rebecca. I shall say : " No, father, I will marry no woman I do not love." Then that will be settled ; my father will let the matter drop. Then I shall tell him about you. Either he will be violent or he will ask me a few questions between his teeth, such as : " How much money have you ? "

Rosa.

Nothing !

RAFAEL.

Or, " What vocation are you master of ? "

ROSA.

The music—if he could only hear—— !

RAFAEL.

My father is as deaf to my art as he is blind. " Are you master of an art, when it will not yield you bread ? " he will say.

ROSA.

. But it will yield you bread, if you will but wait, Rafael !

RAFAEL.

I was very happy when I came through that door. I saw Hanakoff this morning.   He is going to play my Fantasia to-night, Rosa, before the aristocracy ; he is going to let me lead his orchestra !   And in a month he would have played my Symphony !

ROSA.

Would have !   Why not, then ?

RAFAEL.

Why not?   It won't be possible, Rosa.

Rosa.

It must be possible! Why not? Why not?

Rafael.

Well, because the Symphony isn't finished, and in the time when I thought to finish it I shall be working with my hands to keep us from starving—if a man can keep from starving by working with his hands!

Rosa.

Rafael, you shall not tell your father! You shall not sacrifice your career to me. I wounded you too deeply. I didn't mean what I said—I didn't realise what I was doing. See, dear, we must wait for the Symphony. You must go on with your work—you must have peace—you must know that I love you—that I cannot doubt you! Don't you feel that the music will succeed?

Rafael.

It must succeed! It's beautiful. My God, I know it's beautiful! Because it is you, Rosa, shining through my art, lifting up my spirit till I can't call the work mine. It comes from you and from God!

Rosa.

Then, against my will, will you put me between

God and the message he sends to the world through you? No!

RAFAEL.

I must accept the challenge you have made. I am a musician; but I'm a man first!

ROSA.

But—but I——   [*She weeps.*

RAFAEL.

Don't—don't! And this is the day I had looked forward to for so many weary months; my music has found a great man who believes in it, and on that day my spirit is sunken within me; I am waiting to give my father a blow that may kill him, and the woman I love so tenderly is sobbing her foolish little heart out on my knee!

ROSA.

[*Springing up.*] Not now! I have stopped sobbing —the tears have cleared my eyes—I see better than you! I will not have you magnify the doubt I threw into my angry words. There was no doubt; I spoke falsely. Have I not given you my life? I should not dare to doubt you! There are things that must not, shall not be done. We are going to pass through a fire of hatred, scorn, ridicule. We *must* have success, we *must* triumph, and we must protect your father from harm. Go! Tell your father you cannot marry Rebecca ; tell him he must not think of that. Lead him home, speak kind words to him, but don't tell him of me. And then go to work on your Symphony. You say I inspired it. You touch my vanity. I want to inspire it to the end! Don't mind me, don't think of me. Work, work, and only let me once in a while come softly, silently, and——

[She kisses his hand.

RAFAEL.

Rosa! Rosa! How you tempt me! I want to do what is right. I can't tell which it is, but the child of my soul is coming forth into the world, and your kiss is so like a mother's kiss—it seems to bid me be gentle to my child—not to kill it before it is born. Oh, how I love my music—love it because it lets me express my love for you! I say the world shall never forget how I loved you when my music goes down to history! Rosa, Rosa, can you wait—can you trust me?

ROSA.

[*Joyfully.*] You are going to grant my prayer—you're going to wait—wait! I'm so glad—I'm so glad!

Rafael.

Unless they force me to it, I'll wait. I must go
and find my father; it's late already. And then to
the Symphony! Ah, you—you are my Symphony—it
cannot fail! We must have success—and then let
the Ghetto do what it can! I ought to be back in
an hour. Will you steal a moment to let me tell you
how things stand?

Rosa.

Yes! yes! Good-bye! good-bye! Remember, there
is no Rosa—she does not exist!

> [Rafael *shakes his head laughingly; kisses her.
> Exit. She stands smiling and happy.*

A Voice Without.

That was the man; he's going to marry a
Christian!

Rosa.

Oh!

Another Voice.

He's going to marry the Christian servant in his
father's house!

Various Voices.

Oh! Shame! shame! [Rosa *runs to the window.*]
Oh! Oh!

THE SECOND VOICE.

It's a sacrilege !   He's an infidel !

THE THIRD VOICE.

He's a dog !   [*Mingled cries of " Yes, yes !"*

ROSA.

What will they do ?   That girl ! that girl ! she has
told them !

THE FIRST VOICE.

Shall he do this in our teeth and not suffer ?

VARIOUS VOICES.

No, no !

ROSA.

Ah ! they'll stone him ! ˉ Ah !   O God, it might
be the last time he ever touched my lips !

A WOMAN'S VOICE.

Stone him !   Stone him !   He mocks our God !

ROSA.

Ah, Rafael !   What shall I do ?

VARIOUS VOICES.

He does! He's a dog! He insults us all! Out of the Ghetto with him! Come on!

> [*A number of rough men and women charge along the street, and are seen through the window, repeating their cries, which then begin to diminish in the distance.*

ROSA.

It has come! He's alone—he'll face them—he will not yield an inch! [*A rising yell of the mob is heard.*] Rafael! No, he shall not be alone! No! No!

> [*She opens the door. A yell from the mob farther in the distance; she locks the door and runs off past the window. A still more distant yell from the mob dying away.*

END OF THE SECOND ACT.

THE THIRD ACT

SCENE: *A street. At the right the entrance to the synagogue, with steps and a portico. At the left the house of* AARON, *before which are some chairs, in the shade of an awning. Some trees and shrubs give a grateful contrast to the surroundings of* SACHEL'S *house, seen in* ACT I.

The final chant of a Jewish service is heard within the synagogue. Enter REBECCA, *flushed from her interview with* RAFAEL, *as the chant ends, and among others,* AARON *comes out of the synagogue.*

AARON.

Ah, you've come back! Did you find Esther at home?

REBECCA.

No; you knew she would not be at home!

F

AARON.

Eh ! After you had gone, my dear, there I saw her,
going into the synagogue.

Enter ROSA ; *she looks about anxiously.*

Well, how did you—how did you get on ?

REBECCA.

[*Angrily, seeing* ROSA.] I——

AARON.

[*Seeing* ROSA.] 'Sh ! It's all arranged, my girl !
You wanted him ; now you have him. Are you
happy ?

REBECCA.

[*Her eyes on* ROSA, *with growing malevolence.*] Yes.

AARON.

Go in. Rafael is coming here, and the Rabbi—a
quiet talk. Make yourself look well ; the boy's a
little high-strung, you know. By-and-by we will go
out by the shop door ; we will come round this way
and join them. We must use tact. Will you come
in ?

REBECCA.

[*Still facing* ROSA.] In a moment.   [*Exit* AARON.

ROSA.

[*Overcoming a reluctance.*] Have you seen Rafael ?

REBECCA.

He's not here. [*Malignantly.*] He went home again.

ROSA.

Do you speak the truth ?

REBECCA.

If I spoke all the truth I know you would not stay to hear it !

ROSA.

All the truth you know would not take long to tell !   [*Exit.*

REBECCA.

She hates me !   She shall hate me more !
                                    [*Exit into the house.*

Enter SACHEL *and* ESTHER *from the synagogue ; she looks about.*

SACHEL.

You do not see him ?

ESTHER.

Not yet.

SACHEL.

He won't come; he suspects that the Rabbi will try to influence him.

Enter SAMSON *and* DANIEL.

ESTHER.

He said he would walk home with us. Good afternoon, have you seen Rafael?

DANIEL.

Good afternoon. [*To* SAMSON.] *Have* we seen Rafael!

SAMSON.

Is he looking for us?

SACHEL.

He might be; he does not care what vagabond he goes with.

DANIEL.

It is true! For I hear he is about to turn Christian and marry his father's maid-servant!

SAMSON.

And any one who dislikes it is to be thrown out of the house—even if it be his father! Daniel, shall we stay to meet such a person?

DANIEL.

I scorn the interview !   [*Exeunt.*

SACHEL.

You are rascals and liars ! [*To* ESTHER.] They speak the truth !   It is Rosa who has turned my son against me !

ESTHER.

Oh, be still !   Here comes the Rabbi !

Enter THE RABBI, *with a father, a mother, and their son, who seems subdued, as if after an exhortation by* THE RABBI. THE RABBI *dismisses them blandly.*

THE RABBI.

That boy came as stubborn as a donkey, but a little touch of sympathy, enough concession to soothe his pride, a little tact withal, and he departs as meek as a lamb.

SACHEL.

But Rafael is my son, and you cannot twist him about your finger.   He has no heart; he treats me like a dog.   They say he is foul of my maid-servant. If it's true——

THE RABBI.

'Sh ! 'sh !   Scandalous !   Are you every gossip's

plaything ? Come ! Violence, violence—we shall do nothing with violence. Rafael is young, short-sighted and stubborn ; but he's a good fellow at heart. We must handle him delicately, like a big trout. You leave him to me, and he will stay at home and marry Aaron's daughter, willingly.

[*They sit in front of* AARON'S *house.*

ESTHER.

Now what did I tell you, you silly old man !

THE RABBI.

Silly old man ! Not at all. An affectionate father, deeply troubled about his only child—sorely vexed because too many things have gone wrong at once ! Would you have him sit still and not open his mouth ? Oh no, Sachel is not the man to let things take care of themselves !

SACHEL.

It is true ! What does she know about the feelings of a parent ? Ah, I would mould things now, Rabbi, but times have changed. Once, as it is written in the Books of Moses, a son must obey his father, or he would be stoned to the gates of the city ! That was right !

THE RABBI.

It was right then; but, as you so very rightly observe, Sachel, times have changed; and when one throws stones now, one must pay for the windows. So, instead of stoning Rafael, we shall marry him to Rebecca; and in time you shall be the grandfather of a boy; a boy, I say! Ha, ha, ha! You don't laugh enough, Sachel!

SACHEL.

I cannot laugh! I tell you there is a serpent in my house. This girl—this Rosa, I could swear that she——

THE RABBI.

Shame! shame! I won't hear about it! It was for you that I was preaching, but you do not listen when you come to synagogue. Of course, you were thinking about Rafael. You leave him to me. He shall marry Rebecca, do you hear? In such matters as this you are a child!

SACHEL.

He shall do my bidding, or he shall go in rags! 'Sh!

> [*They all listen. Enter* RAFAEL, *with his hand bound up carelessly in a handkerchief.*

THE RABBI.

Why, it's Rafael! What an unexpected pleasure!

RAFAEL.

It *is* a long time since I have seen you.

SACHEL.

Daniel and Samson are liars! But if it were true, I would——

THE RABBI.

Tut, tut! What's the matter? Mumbling about business matters on the Sabbath! Well, well, how you've shot up since—since——

RAFAEL.

Since last I came to the synagogue I have had time to grow.

THE RABBI.

I pass that over. I don't look upon you as gone astray. You are seeking for the light, and when you find it, whether you think so now or not, you will find it there! [*Indicating the synagogue.*] Just as when you find happiness you will find it here.

RAFAEL.

In the house of Aaron?

The Rabbi.

With your father, and at home, under the
roof where your mother lived. Ah! what a fine
career is open to you in following out your father's
business! It isn't every boy who has such oppoitu-
nities!

Rafael.

Business! You in your synagogue—you ought to
be the enemy of business. You ought to preach it
to our people without end that their life of morning,
noon, and night, and not a breath drawn but for sake
of gain, is a sickly mockery of life, and that it is
against the law of Moses!

The Rabbi.

Another prophet! Business, gain, contrary to the
laws of Moses! Go on, my boy! Let us have the
sermon you would preach! Ha, ha! Go on! Now
I shall learn something.

Rafael.

Have I not read in the Book of Moses how the
people divided the soil, and there was no one who had
more than another; and there was no grinding of the
poor, and there was never any selling of lands: " For
mine is the soil, and you are but strangers unto

Me!"   And among them was not business despised?
How did Jacob speak of Issachar?

The Rabbi.

Bravo!   "A   strong   ass,"   eh?   Ha, ha, ha!
You've been deep in the Pentateuch.   Where will you
find   such   inspirations   in   any   other   Sacred   Book?
But you should read them under guidance, you foolish
boy!

Rafael.

Under guidance!   There is a guidance born in me
that takes me where I am, and I do not fear!   It is
a guidance that lives to-day; it is not a guidance dug
from the bones of a dead people of the dim past!   I
know.   You are going to say that Solomon did business,
that David did business.   I don't care if they did!
And you tell me that I skim the surface, that I miss
the spirit of the Jewish faith; and I tell you that it
is this spirit that my soul revolts against—the spirit
that holds our people in chains—the chains of the
Ghetto!

The Rabbi.

Ghetto!   There is no Ghetto!   We do not live in
Ghettos now, my boy!   Preposterous!

RAFAEL.

And now *you* are skimming the surface, and *you* will not see the truth that underlies! You say there is no Ghetto! Could I ever play with any but another Jew when I was a child? Could I ever eat with a Christian? Was I ever taught by any but a Jew? No, you have taught me to despise the Christians!

THE RABBI.

They persecuted us for ages; they have not taught us to admire them.

RAFAEL.

They have ceased to persecute us, they have taken down the stones of the Ghetto walls, but still we are taught to despise them; still we try to think ourselves the chosen people. We set ourselves as a race against them and the universal brotherhood of man. This is the proof of it: *our women we marry, theirs we pay!*

THE RABBI.

That is not true; it's a shameful calumny!

RAFAEL.

I can pick you ten young men to prove it—out of those that heard you preach to-day!

The Rabbi.

How dare you say such a thing! Are you a Jew no longer? Am I speaking to a Christian?

Rafael.

You are speaking to a Jew who claims to-day and to-morrow as his own—not yesterday! A Jew who believes that it shall not be asked if a man worship in a synagogue or in a cathedral, in a chapel or in a mosque, or in silence and solitude under God's own dome! And the falsehood you have brought me up by; our hatred and our bigotry which keeps us away from them, our cursed earthiness which keeps them away from us—I loathe it all—I hate it—I will fight it as long as I live! I am a Jew—a Jew of to-day and to-morrow; and every man whom God created in his image is my brother!

The Rabbi.

The boy's gone daft! Daft!

Sachel.

No, not that; he's been poisoned—poisoned by this damned creature in my house! She's his——

The Rabbi.

Be still! I lost my self-control—set me a better

example. I—I—it is many years—indeed, I may say
I have never listened to such a tirade ! Let me tell
you, you will live to regret what you have said here
in the very shadow of the synagogue. I will not
treat it seriously ; I cannot ! That you—a mere
boy who has gobbled a bit here and a bit there from
the Book of Law, should have the monstrous effrontery
to—to——

RAFAEL.

Father, are you ready to walk home now ?

SACHEL.

I—I am not rested yet.   [*He pokes* THE RABBI.

RAFAEL.

From the sermon ?

*Enter two rough fellows, supporting another, who has
a swollen eye ; they stand at a distance, with sinister
looks at* RAFAEL.

SACHEL.

Ha, ha ! [*Pokes* THE RABBI.] You don't laugh
enough !

THE RABBI.

As I was about to say, when I was interrupted,
you have said that Rafael wants to go away. Then

let him go! When he comes back he'll have a
different view of his people. Do you fear he won't
come back; not come back to his home—to his blind
old father? You are foolish, Sachel! Drive him
away, and he'll find that there is no home in the
world like a Jewish home—that a clock ticks nowhere
in the world as it does by one's own hearth. Ah,
the Christians don't know what family life is; they
have nothing to compare with ours. It is because
we stay by one another, because we are sober and
temperate and industrious and respectful of our
elders!

> [RAFAEL *goes up, faces the three men at the back;
> they slink off. He returns, showing a new
> determination in his face.*

SACHEL.

He ought to marry; then he would appreciate
that.

THE RABBI.

Marry? Who spoke of marrying? He doesn't
want to marry yet; I wouldn't have him marry yet.
Don't try to hurry Rafael; he's not the fellow to
stand it. My dear friends, when the time comes, and
a strong, fine-looking young fellow makes up his
mind that——

RAFAEL.

It is a good idea.   I have been thinking of marriage all day.

SACHEL.

Eh, you have?   Now what sort of thoughts did you have?   I suppose you thought I would object, eh?

ESTHER.

But he doesn't know any girls.   He never looks at them !

RAFAEL.

I know one.

ESTHER.

Indeed !   And whom, pray ?

RAFAEL.

Aaron's daughter—Rebecca.   Do you know her ?
                    [SACHEL *nudges* THE RABBI.

ESTHER.

This is where she lives ; and she came to see us yesterday, with her father.

RAFAEL.

Indeed !   What did he come for ?

ESTHER.

To sell some wool! She's a fine girl, I should say.

RAFAEL.

A delicate person—a retiring person—a shrinking person!

ESTHER.

Oh, not too much so.

RAFAEL.

[*As if disappointed.*] Then you think she is not so sensitive a creature?

ESTHER.

Well, I should say she *was* perhaps rather sensitive.

THE RABBI.

Shrinking, I should say.

SACHEL.

Shrinking; she is shrinking, I should say!

[*A pause.*

ESTHER.

Well——

THE RABBI.

And ——-

SACHEL.

And did——?

RAFAEL.

Eh? Rain—rain? Oh no!

THE RABBI.

Speaking of Rebecca reminds me, and I will tell you an anecdote——

RAFAEL.

Curious coincidence that, just as my mind was full of thoughts of love and matrimony, in should burst this same Rebecca!

SACHEL.

Eh? eh?   [*He nudges* THE RABBI.

THE RABBI.

Curious? Not at all! Beauty, health, cleverness —the idea is in the air, wherever she goes. If I were a young man—but such matters are not for my concern until they are brought to the synagogue—I should——

    [REBECCA *appears at the window of* AARON'S *house.*

RAFAEL.

True, Rabbi, true! And you do wisely not to meddle with them. Do you know there was   faint

G

suggestion in the air—like the subtle odour of some tender flower—that possibly Rebecca would not be averse to marrying me !

SACHEL.

Well, well, well !   Hee, hee !

> [*He nudges* THE RABBI.

ESTHER.

Dear me ; love at first sight !

RAFAEL.

Not at first sight ; we have had previous interviews——

SACHEL.

Eh ? eh ?   The rascal !

RAFAEL.

——about fourteen years ago.   And now we have met again, and I thought she would be willing to marry me, but being so shrinking a creature, like— what shall I say—like a snail withdrawing into its shell——   [REBECCA *draws back in pain.*

ESTHER.

[*Mildly deprecating.*] Oh !

RAFAEL.

She would not say so in as many words.

[REBECCA *looks out again.*

ESTHER.

I am sorry for the poor girl; for, if the truth be told— But, there, you are not serious about anything!

SACHEL.

Why do you say "poor girl" when she would bring——

THE RABBI.

But Rafael doesn't look to dowries; he has a romantic turn.   The fact that she would bring five or six thousand guilders——

SACHEL.

Ten thousand guilders !

RAFAEL.

Ten thousand guilders ! [*In irony.*] H'm!   But— Oh, well, I'm not a very keen observer, Rabbi; it is probable that Rebecca never——

THE RABBI.

On the contrary.   For, speaking of that very matter, which, of course, is no affair of mine, she——

RAFAEL.

Quite true, quite true! What did you say, aunt?

ESTHER.

Eh? Oh, I was going to say that she begged your photograph of me yesterday, and when it dropped into the canal she was almost ready to cry.

RAFAEL.

H'm! But it was careless of her to drop me into that nasty canal!

SACHEL.

It blew in; there came a great gust of wind.

RAFAEL.

The wind must have been Aaron, disputing the value of his wool!

THE RABBI.

Good! Good! Ha, ha, ha! He has a mind; he will not let his heart run away with his head!

RAFAEL.

And so Rebecca—— H'm! But I shall not let

my heart run away with my purse. I should hold
my hot young blood in bounds!

SACHEL.

Not always! Not always! A young man 'must
have his day!

RAFAEL.

But is she well? Is she sound? One cannot be
too cautious. I knew of a girl who seemed as strong
as a green peach on a tree; and she had not been two
days married when, what do you think? Why, she
died! She knew she was going to die, but she
never told him! That's awful, awful! Oh! Oh!
I could not stand a thing like that! [THE RABBI
rises to look at RAFAEL's *face.*] I have a soul, Rabbi,
I know, because you taught me so, and a deception
like that—it would kill my love.

[REBECCA *draws in, distressed.*

THE RABBI.

Are you serious?

RAFAEL.

Am I serious? He asks me if I am serious! But
that was not Rebecca. You think Rebecca is——

THE RABBI.

She's as honest as her father!

RAFAEL.

Ah! Two of them, as honest as each other! [THE RABBI *has growing appreciation of the irony.*] H'm! But a good housewife? A good needlewoman? Sharp over the counter? My father has not slaved to feed the idleness of another man's daughter!

ESTHER.

I'll answer for that. I thought I could bake cakes, but she's coming to-morrow to teach me how! You never tasted such cakes!

THE RABBI.

Indeed, I believe I have heard them spoken of.

SACHEL.

[*Who has been musing.*] Eh—cakes? You cannot expect a girl to know everything. Anyway, she's coming to-morrow; and Esther is going to——

RAFAEL.

Esther is going to learn from her. Excellent!

SACHEL.

Eh? [*He is nudged by* ESTHER.] Yes, yes!

RAFAEL.

Good, good! I half suspect that—that you look with favour on Rebecca. We—we had considerable conversation this morning, we talked of money—and love—and——

SACHEL.

They talked of love! Now, what did you say of love?

RAFAEL.

And we talked of money—and of children—and of —money.

[ESTHER *looks at* THE RABBI; *she also now in dawning suspicion of* RAFAEL'S *irony.*

SACHEL.

Ha, ha! They talked of love and children! Of love and children! We must have some wine, Rafael —this is the house of a friend. Esther, you go and fetch it. Now what——

ESTHER.

They charge two prices at that place around the corner.

SACHEL.

I say we will have some wine! Some good wine Go

ESTHER.

Very well; it is a season of denial with us.

THE RABBI.

But the extreme heat! [*Whispers.*] Get some from
my house.   [*Exit* ESTHER.

SACHEL.

H'm! They talked of children and love! And
what did you say about children, my boy? Ah, they
are beautiful things; though I could not see one, I
could fondle it! What about children, my boy?

RAFAEL.

We said that they should each have two cradles;
one with a soft pillow of burnt wool and one with a
hard pillow of burnt cotton, so that they should learn
the difference before they were old enough to tell the
sun from a silver coin.

[*An angry gesture from* THE RABBI.

SACHEL.

Eh, what— H'm! Yes, yes, but later—later
would do as well. And about love, Rafael; what did
she say about love?

RAFAEL.

Oh, she is a shrinking creature—as shrinking as

wool unmixed with cotton! And, at first, she would
not talk of love, but at length she said that when
she was married she expected to have a dozen——

SACHEL.

A dozen! That's too large a family in such times
as these!

RAFAEL.

A dozen of everything.

SACHEL.

Ah yes—a dozen of everything, Rafael; a dozen
of the finest. Her father has told me so.

Enter ESTHER, *followed by a servant with glasses
of wine on a tray.*

And a dowry of ten thousand guilders! What do you
think of that, my boy? The wine—here! I shall
propose a toast! [*He takes a glass and gives glasses
to the others;* ESTHER *and* THE RABBI *take theirs
unwillingly.*] Here! Here!

THE RABBI.

[*Holding his glass toward* RAFAEL.] I suggest a toast
to an open heart—to a tongue that leads no man astray!

Rafael.

Hear! The Rabbi suggests that—with *his* tongue! I'll drink that toast with *you*, Rabbi!

Sachel.

It is my wine! I am proposing the toast! I——

The Rabbi.

[*To* Sachel.] You had better drink in silence, and go home. You are deceiving yourself: you know not where you stand!

Rafael.

What! What does he mean, father? Am I deceiving myself? Are you not planning to marry me to Rebecca? Do you fear, then, that I have fallen in love with her? Is she not an honest girl—a shrinking girl—a girl as good as Father Aaron?

Sachel.

Yes, and better!

Rafael.

Will she not bring me a dozen of everything, and ten thousand guilders? Could man ask more? What's wrong here? Why do they not raise their glasses?

SACHEL.

Because they will not let me manage my own affairs! He is my son, not yours! It is my wine, not yours! Drink, then, drink to Rebecca, the richest girl in the Ghetto, a beautiful young girl, a marvellous young girl——

[ESTHER *turns appealingly to* THE RABBI; *both look on in distress and perplexity.*

RAFAEL.

But they do not raise their glasses, father; they will not drink, father! Why? Do they see handwriting on the wall? Do they think I have forsaken my race? Do they think I have given my heart and soul to the heart and soul of another? Why do they not raise their glasses?

SACHEL.

Let them throw it on the ground if they will! Every one tries to thwart me, every one but you; but they shall not! I am Sachel! Drink with me! Drink to Rebecca, your wife, Rafael! For this day I have seen Aaron; I have sat with him—yesterday and to-day I have sat with him! I have laboured with him, my boy; your father was not wanting! He would have squirmed into my house with eight thousand; but I raised him! I raised him two thousand, my boy! We have agreed, agreed! She is yours, Rafael—yours! To Rebecca, my daughter-in-law! Now will you drink—will you clink your glasses? [*He reaches about; no one clinks; RAFAEL turns away and pours his wine on the ground.*] Where are you? I'm all alone! What's the matter? What's the matter?

RAFAEL.

· They have not touched their glasses, father! They stand staring at you, without words!

ESTHER.

Sachel, come home!

SACHEL.

What do you mean? You fools, what do I care what you mean! He's going to stay at home and be my boy, my comfort, my staff in my old age; he's going to marry Rebecca! Rafael and Rebecca! Rafael and Rebecca! Does it not sound beautiful—beautiful!

Enter AARON *by way of the street, dragging* REBECCA *by the hand; she holds back in deep mortification.*

AARON.

Ha, ha! It does! It does!

REBECCA.

Father !

AARON.

Don't be afraid, my girl. [*To the others.*] I suspected what you were doing ! Rafael—[*effusively*]—since the day she was born I've had an eye on you! Eh, what's the matter ? Why are you all so glum ?

RAFAEL.

[*He goes to the table and gets a glass, then back.*] On this solemn occasion, sir, I was about to propose a toast.

SACHEL.

Yes.

AARON.

[*Goes to table.*] We'll drink it here.

> [*He offers the glass to* REBECCA.

REBECOA.

I don't want to drink, father; I want to go in, father !

AARON.

Bosh ! What are you afraid of ? Speak on, my boy !

SACHEL.

Yes, speak on, and speak your soul to them ! They

need not think to thwart this marriage! Let them beware!

AARON.

[*Surprised.*] What's this about?

RAFAEL.

It's about my soul—my soul that leaps its bounds at last—my soul that speaks from the heart of a man! [*A passer-by at the back stops to listen.*] My soul that dwelt in the wilderness—a rumbling, roaring, raging, lying, sweating wilderness of traffic in the things of earth—my soul in the wilderness crying in vain, in vain, for the love of another soul like mine. Is it not so, Rebecca?

AARON.

Hear, hear!

REBECCA.

Let me go, father!

RAFAEL.

Let *me* go, father; let *me* go! I would not be slain on the altar, father! The knife is in my flesh! This is the blood of my heart! O God, crieth my soul in vain ? Where—where is the angel that shall stay my father's hand ?

[*A crowd slowly gathers.*

AARON.

Masterly! Masterly! Here she is! What an auctioneer he would make!

RAFAEL.

What an auctioneer I should make! Ah! [*He runs and stands on the synagogue steps.*] My father bids me sell my soul! Shall I sell it cheap—my soul and my heart's blood? Shall it be knocked down to the solitary thirsty first who bids? I, to whom the stench of avarice is the breath of morning and night —I, who have seen a man sell his soul on the scales——

SACHEL.

What does he mean by that ?

RAFAEL.

I—to be knocked down for two pink lips and a banknote! See—my red heart's blood! See—see— see! And you would have me sell it for ten thousand pieces of silver! And I say no! no! no!

AARON.

He wants more! Oh! I will not give it, do you hear? It is an insult to ask more—an insult to my daughter!

REBECCA.

Father, come away!

ESTHER.

Sachel, come home!

SACHEL.

Let me be! What does he want? What does he mean?

AARON.

Ha, ha! he wants more!

RAFAEL.

I want more! The sale shall be public! [*The crowd thickens.*] I will have my price. Who bids more? Who bids? What do you bid, my girl?

REBECCA.

Nothing—nothing— I——   [*Exit.*

RAFAEL.

She bids all she has, and yet I will not take it!
More—more—who bids me more?

AARON.

Ha, ha! ten million guilders, idiot!

Enter ROSA, *at the back.*

RAFAEL.

He bids ten million guilders, and that is still too
small.   You bid nothing but money, money; have
you nothing else?   Who comes?   Who bids?   Who
bids?   See, see— [*He points to* ROSA, *who has
worked forward, pressed by the crowd.*] Another
bidder!   Another bidder!   The angel—the angel
come to stay my father's hand!

[ESTHER *and others turn fiercely on* ROSA.

ROSA.

[*Panic-stricken, pressed by the crowd.*]   Rafael!
Rafael!

SACHEL.

It's Rosa!   It's Rosa!

RAFAEL.

Rosa, Rosa, what do you bid? They bid money, nothing but money; and you—you——

ROSA.

[*Wringing her hands.*] Rafael!

SACHEL.

She calls him Rafael! A curse! A damning curse!   [*The crowd murmurs.*

RAFAEL.

Silence! It is my blood we are drinking! It is my soul we are selling! [*To* AARON.] And you bid more than all you have, and yet it will not do; and you, Rosa, angel—angel—for my heart—for my soul —bid, bid!

ROSA.

For your heart—my heart! For your soul—my soul!

RAFAEL.

Ha, ha! Going! Going!

THE RABBI.

Going the way of the profligate—to the damned!
            [*Exit into the synagogue, closing the doors.*

RAFAEL.

Gone to the highest bidder! She has been my wife for months! [SACHEL *sinks into a chair ; hisses and groans from the crowd.*] Now let the Ghetto damn me if it can !

ONE OF THE CROWD.

She's a Christian !

[*The crowd surround* RAFAEL, *who holds them at bay.*]

END OF THE THIRD ACT.

THE FOURTH ACT

SCENE: *The same as* ACT I. *It is seven days later.*
AARON *discovered at the door; he holds some letters
in his hand.*

AARON.

I had rather talk to you here.

Enter SACHEL, *pale, bowed and trembling; the two
sit on a bench at the right.*

Then it is true that you have not heard from Rafael
for a week? What happened that day, after the
officers had dispersed the crowd?

SACHEL.

[*With a sob, then restraining his emotions.*] He
brought her back here to get the few things that
belong to her. He said that as soon as he had done
with Hanakoff he would come and get her. Then
he went away. He said he would be back in the

morning; and he has been gone a week! My God, it
was I who made him so anxious to leave—it is the
judgment of the Almighty upon my sins!

AARON.

[*Calculatingly, as he looks at the letters in his hand.*]
Oh, he's your son; I fancy if he got in the vicinity of
harm, he saw it before it saw him! And the girl,
why do you let her stay here?

SACHEL.

The Rabbi! The Rabbi came here and made me
promise to keep the girl until Rafael could find a
home for her. I thought it would be the next day;
I promised. The Rabbi said he repented the strong
words he had uttered when he slammed the door of
the synagogue. H'm! The Rabbi is not much better
than you, or at least, than me! The only difference
is that the Rabbi is always repenting! If Rafael
would only come back, I'd let him keep the girl here
for ever—what do I care! I want my son—the only
thing I live for!

AARON.

But doesn't the girl know where he is?

SACHEL.

No, no. Esther kept telling me that Rosa has had

no word from Rafael. I would not believe it; and this morning I took hold of her; I cursed her up and down for not telling me where he was. She said if she knew where he was she would walk to him, if it was a thousand miles, rather than stay another night under my roof. Then, for the third time this week, she had a fit of hysterics—I never heard such sobs in all my life! When she quieted down she went up and put on the rags she first came here in; and since then she has refused to take food from us; she won't enter the house; she is wandering about here somewhere now. I don't know; though she be a Christian and a pauper, I suppose I'll have to accept her for my daughter-in-law, if he'll only come!

AARON.

She, that broke up your home and took your son away from the finest young woman in the Ghetto? She, that robbed him of his faith and brought him to a pass where every one is saying that he has run away rather than face the consequences of his acts? H'm!

SACHEL.

What am I going to do? If he's dead, I *will* keep her! Isn't she the only one in the world whose sorrow will approach mine?

AARON.

But if he is not dead? If he comes back? [*Circumspectly makes as if to open one of the letters.*] Look here—

> [*Enter the* RABBI; AARON *hastily puts away the letters.*

Oh, the Rabbi! [*Whispers.*] We must get rid of him. I want to talk to you.

RABBI.

Good evening! How is that girl? Is she still crying her eyes out? It's pitiful! It is dangerous! I must see her! [AARON *nudges* SACHEL.

SACHEL.

She's all right. I have not heard her stir since she went to bed.

RABBI.

Oh, she's gone to bed—good! Sachel, Rafael had my promise to protect that girl; and I will protect her. Last Saturday we were all overwrought; we were taken by surprise. But now that we all realise it, it comes to this: Rafael has married a Christian girl; she knows what an affront this is to the religion in which Rafael was reared, and to which inevitably he must return his full devotion when he grows an older and wiser man. Now there is but one remedy: Rosa must become a Jewess. Not to-night or to-morrow; but she must be influenced to open her heart to the faith of her husband; and she must be urged to welcome a future day when she shall enter the synagogue and come forth from there with all the hatred, all the revulsion which she has seen in our faces to-day, buried for ever! Teach her to be thankful that this is Holland, where a Christian *may* become a Jewess.

AARON.

Rabbi, your sentiments are worthy of your calling. Sachel and I have been talking; we both regret our bitter words of that day. Sachel has become reconciled—as much as any Jew could. And, to tell the truth, we had gone so far as to dismiss the subject and to devote ourselves to a very important matter of business which had to go over from Friday.

THE RABBI.

I see—I see! I am very glad, then! We must make Rosa understand the things that are glorious in our religion; the inspirations that have sustained us through centuries of the bitterest persecution that

men have ever known.   And she must believe that
we shall cling to them until that supreme day when
Jerusalem is peopled anew with the race which God
has chosen for His own.   Is it not so?

SACHEL.

Yes, yes!   And we'll walk a little way with you.
Then, Aaron, you can come back, and we can go on
with that business.

[*They go up* : THE RABBI *stops at the bridge.*

THE RABBI.

Very well; but you will treat the young girl
tenderly, my friends?   Look here; you and Esther
and Rafael bring her to my house some night when
there will be no one else there.   We'll let her feel
the warmth of our hearts, as if she were already a
Jewess.   We will show her what the inner life of the
Jews is; the life that the Christians have no concep-
tion of.   And so we will work upon her better nature;
but—yes, yes, I see you are busy.   You are not
worrying about Rafael, then?

AARON.

Oh, he'll be all right.   I'm sure of it.

[*They start off over the bridge.*

The Rabbi.

I'm glad to see you here, Aaron. It does you credit to forget your disappointments! [*Exeunt.*

A bell tolls ten o'clock. Enter Rosa. *Her pallor and the tremor of her voice show the effects of intense emotional strain.*

Rosa.

The very hour that he went away, and seven days are gone! Seven days—and he stood here and took me in his arms! Oh!—[*turning*]—you who cry after me that Rafael has deserted his Christian mistress; it is because you never knew the love of anything but money! You look down—always down! But the same clear sky was over our heads when he kissed me here, and we looked up to it and thanked God, who made us dare to lead our life in open truth before the world! Let *God* punish us for loving each other, if that be a crime! Oh, *does* He punish us? Where is my Rafael, you star that watched over us then! I love him, I love him; I cannot live without him— sweet star, tell me where he is to-night! Oh, it is from pity that you will not tell! And he lies cold and dead! Rafael, Rafael, I'm all alone—all alone! [*Weeps.*] No, no; it can't be that! Dear God, who sees me here among these aliens, you could not be so cruel to your own ! Not so cruel as that ! Not so cruel as that ! [*She sobs ; exit.*

Enter AARON *and* SACHEL.

AARON.

Where is Esther ?

SACHEL.

Can't you hear her snoring ? I can, though she is away at the back of the house ! I have not slept seven hours in these seven days !

AARON.

Do you think the girl has any suspicion that Rafael may have found that he has undertaken the impossible ? If he did throw her off—I don't say that he has—but if he did, it must strike her that she wouldn't have a place to go in all the world !

SACHEL.

She believes in him.

AARON.

When he is with her, yes ! But when he is away, and she waits and waits, are not all women alike ? Doesn't she know that he has sacrificed every guilder that he might have had from you ?

SACHEL.

I said that to them.   Why did I not hold my cursed
tongue!   He hadn't a copper in his pocket ; the
poor boy had given away everything he had, to bury
Mordecai's son.

AARON.

And does not she know that he gave up every friend
he had, too, when he forsook his religion ?   These
things must have passed through her mind.

SACHEL.

What do I care what is passing in *her* mind !

AARON.

Of course, of course !   [*Pulls the letters from his
pocket.*]   But the main probability is that Rafael will
soon return.   I am only thinking whether before he
returns this girl could not be influenced to leave here,
made to believe that the boy has deserted her ?   You
can't blame me for considering my daughter's feelings
in this matter.   Now suppose we could let drop a few
things in Rosa's presence, without appearing to know
that she overheard ?

SACHEL.

I don't care about her !   I want *him* to come back.

AARON.

Don't you see: after a whole week, after all her waiting and waiting, without a word from him and with her whole life trembling in the balance, then if she overhears certain things——! Of course if we try to persuade her he is gone, she'll suspect at once. But there are certain remarks that we can let drop, quite casually, you know, that will absolutely make her believe that he does not intend to come back; that he has deserted her.

SACHEL.

But she *won't* believe it!

AARON.

No, not if we try to convince her! But we won't try! You only make certain statements within her hearing; and if she says they are not true, just shrug your shoulders! What is in that girl's mind? Either that he has met harm, or that he is afraid to come back to her; that the poverty staring him in the face has been too much for him. Seven days is a long time when a woman is alone on the rack of doubt. Now, do you see what I mean?

Sachel.

But I want my son! I don't care whether he marries your daughter! I want my son!

Aaron.

[*Tapping the letters.*] Here are some letters. One for you and four for Rosa.

Sachel.

Where did *you* get them? Is mine from Rafael? Yes? Ah, ah! Read it, quick!

Aaron.

[*Reads.*] "Father: Rosa will tell you where I am. I am your son; do not be harsh to Rosa. The Rabbi told me that he knew you would keep her over night; as I left her for a night, relying upon his good offices with you, so I feel I may leave her for a week. Good-bye, father. Rafael."

Sachel.

He's all right! He's all right! [*Pauses, suddenly.*] Look here, you miserable rascal, you've had this for a week. You've bribed that postman; it's a crime!

Aaron.

One for you and four for her. Will you listen to

'one of those he wrote to her? [*Opens it.*] Shall I open it?

SACHEL.

You have, already.

AARON.

Shall I read it?

SACHEL.

[*After hesitation.*] Yes.

AARON.

[*Reads.*] "My darling: If I take ship at once with Hanakoff for London, I have the opportunity of a life time; it will fix me in my career as I had never dreamed of. My mind tells my heart that I must go; but I am as joyful as I am sorrowful; for in a week, dear, I take you away from the stifling air you breathe to-night—out of the Ghetto, into the freedom which is the right of our love. Good night, my angel! Your Rafael."

SACHEL.

He'll have money now. He'll never look at me again. She's got him! She's got him! O, I would to my Maker I were dead!

AARON.

No, no! She hasn't got him! She shan't have him! Don't you see, this clears the way for the very thing I proposed to you.

SACHEL.

What? What? It might succeed, with the girl in the state she is. But if it does, what will Rafael say, to-morrow?

AARON.

Eh? Why, if he finds her gone and she left no word, let him draw his own conclusions; that she was afraid to stand by him; afraid to share his poverty. You say "to-morrow"? He may be back to-night! It's your one chance. If it succeeds, the girl goes, with two hundred guilders in her pocket; Rafael stays home—in due time marries Rebecca—becomes a successful Jew. If it fails—then this Christian robs you of him anyway! [SACHEL *ponders; then suddenly touches him; they listen;* AARON *whispers.*] Only casually; not an effort to convince her! She can't help believing it, then!

SACHEL.

Sh—!

Enter ROSA, *by the bridge; she drops her hands, hopelessly, and stays near the bridge, turned away from them.*

AARON.

[*Without looking about, whispers.*] Was that her step? [SACHEL *nods; a pause;* AARON *begins in a moderate tone.*] Yes; but a man who gives his word to one girl and then deserts her, would desert another girl. Shall I let my daughter risk that? No!

SACHEL.

But I tell you it is not a parallel case! A marriage solemnised in a synagogue is one thing; but a marriage such as this—which we all know is not a marriage, either inside or outside the Ghetto—I tell you it's totally different!

AARON.

Didn't he commit himself morally? Very well! Then he goes and finds that he has been tricked by a venial under-magistrate, for the sake of thirty guilders; and he finds that it was no marriage at all! The girl is reduced merely to the position of his mistress——

I

SACHEL.

Well, doesn't that dispose of *her* ?   Doesn't that rid him of responsibility ?

AARON.

Yes; but it is a high moral consideration that occupies me.   The boy found that he could rid himself of his burden ; the discovery came when he had been looking about for a week, and finding nothing but poverty, privation and despair on every side ; no one would lend him money ; none of his former friends would speak to him ; there was only the choice between an absolutely hopeless struggle and running away.   He ran !   And I say a young man who has thus been tried and found wanting is no man to be my daughter's husband !

SACHEL.

O !   Because Rafael has had one mistress is he not good enough to be your daughter's husband ?

ROSA.

What do you mean !   What do you mean, Sachel ! [*The two men rise, affecting surprise.*]   It is a lie !   It is a cruel lie !

AARON.

Eh ?   Doesn't the *girl* know about it ?

Rosa.

What do you mean by saying that he ran away from me? How do you know that he ran away from me? Where is he! Tell me where he is! Quick, you shall!

Aaron.

No one will know where he is until he has spent the money he sent for. And that ought to keep him a year, even in England.

Rosa.

England—you say he has gone to England? You tell me he has deserted me? After what he said before the synagogue? I say it's a lie—a preposterous lie! It isn't true that I am only his mistress—it's a lie!

Aaron.

I'll tell you what *is* true; after this escapade with you he'll have to prove himself a man before he marries my daughter.

Rosa.

He can't marry your daughter! He's mine! O, God, what does this mean? Can't you find him? Can't you let me see him? He would have written to me—I know he would! Sachel, let me go to him. Sachel, tell me where he is!

AARON.

What could Sachel do, even if he could reach the boy ? After seven days, at the very moment Sachel has been persuaded to accept all this—to treat you as his daughter—here slinks Rafael along the canal and up through the warehouse and whispers that he has given you up! Then he wheedles his father out of more money than I would give ten sons, and then boards a ship for England ! [*To* SACHEL.] Do you think I'll see my daughter marry such a man ? If he wants to return next year on the hope of marrying Rebecca, you tell him to remain in England !

ROSA.

It's a lie ! He couldn't desert me. He's a man of soul—of honour ! It isn't true. My God, it can't be true !

AARON.

You'd better find a place to sleep, and then compose yourself to make the best of it. I have a friend in the country who will receive you. With the money that Rafael has persuaded his father to give you, begin life over again. Come !   [*Touches her.*

ROSA.

No, I will not come ! It is a lie. You try to

convince me because you know I will kill myself
—because you——

AARON.

Has any one tried to convince you? Sachel is the
only one to gain by your going. Has he tried to
convince you?

ROSA.

I know—I know—O God! Sachel, Sachel, as you
fear your God, swear to me that he has deserted me!
Swear to me that he wants to marry Rebecca!

SACHEL.

I—I——

AARON. —

Shall *I* take an oath, on the Law of Moses, that is
fastened to the lintel there?

ROSA.

I will not believe *you* on any oath! I will only
believe Sachel—Sachel, who could not deceive me—
[*turns to* SACHEL]—because you know that if you
make me go away and kill myself Rafael will hate
you, for ever and ever! Sachel, Sachel, can't we get
him back? I'll do anything—anything. I'll become
a Jewess if you'll get him back! Sachel, Sachel!

[*Cries hysterically.*

Aaron.

The poor girl want's your oath. That's a simple matter. [*To* Sachel.] There is no reason why I should stay here to witness this. Good-night!

[*Exit by the bridge.*

Sachel.

Such as you to kill yourself—h'm! Now take your money and be off! I'm going to lock my door.

Rosa.

You haven't said the marriage was false! *You* haven't said he went away! *You* haven't said he wants to marry her—you dare not! It can't be true! It *can't* be true!

Sachel.

Dare not—dare not. What do you mean? You thankless hussy! You wreck my home, you rob me of my son, and then when he has gone and I offer you money to leave me in peace you dare to say I lie!

Rosa.

No, I did not say *you* lied, because *you* have not said that he is deserting me! You will not! You dare not! He loves me; he is coming back! I will stay until he comes!

SACHEL.

He wants to be rid of you. He has gone to England. He wants Aaron to——

ROSA.

Sachel, Sachel, think what you are saying! Tell me he is dead—tell me anything but that he's left me! O, could your son dishonour me? Think what you are saying! No, no—not unless you swear it in the sight of God! Sachel, Sachel—[*as he puts hand on the lintel*]—don't swear to it—[*on her knees*]—don't swear to it!

SACHEL.

[*With a burst of raje.*] God!— Hear me then. You have been nothing but Rafael's mistress! Rafael has deserted you! Rafael wants to marry Rebecca! Rafael has sailed from Amsterdam! By the sacred Law of Moses, by all that is holy in the sight of God, I swear it! I swear it! Now go! Take your money and go! [*She goes towards the canal.*

ROSA.

And so—and so— Dear God—dear God!

SACHEL.

Where are you? Here, take it—take it! Where are you going?

· Rosa.

[*At the canal.*] Dear God—dear God— No more
—no more!

Sachel.

Come away!

Rosa.

Rafael!   [*She jumps into the canal.*

Sachel.

Stop! O—O God! It isn't true! Rosa! Rosa!
[*At the wall.*] A stick! A stick! I cannot find one!
Where are you? For God's sake, answer! Don't
you hear? O God! O God! [*Turns to the house,
where music is being played.*] Daniel! Samson!
Open the door! [*The music drowns his voice.*] Help!
help! [*He rushes back.*] Rosa! Reach out your hand!
Where are you—where are you? Answer me—[*the
music ceases abruptly*]—answer. [*A silence. He slinks
away from the wall. A pause.*] What will Rafael
do? What will God do?

[*He hears the footsteps of* Rafael.

Enter Rafael, *joyously.*

Rafael.

Hello, father, father! I'm home again! Why
haven't I heard from you? I—what's the matter?

SACHEL.

[*Trembling.*] I—I—don't mind me! I—I—I thought you wouldn't come back. We didn't get your letters until to-day. But you've come—you've come! Rafael, for God's sake, don't leave me! For God's sake—I'm sick, I'm blind, I've only a little while left! Stay with me. Don't leave me alone— you mustn't leave me alone!

RAFAEL.

You are not well. Have you been in the heat? Father, why do you tremble so?

SACHEL.

I'm not trembling, my boy. I—I—my boy, my boy, ask me anything and I will give it to you! I can't live without my son! If you speak a harsh word to me I shall drop dead, Rafael.

RAFAEL.

Father, father, be calm; Heaven knows I don't want to be harsh to you; there's a clean page to begin on if you like. We'll leave this place; come and live with Rosa and me. She has never spoken a harsh word to you, has she? Don't you see now that she has the gentleness of an angel ?   Wait till our people know her !

SACHEL.

Yes, yes, I know; my God, I know—I—I—[RAFAEL *makes as if to go in.*] Rafael, for God's sake, don't leave me!

RAFAEL.

Where is she, father ?   She was afraid to stay here; but I told her she was my wife, and that you loved your son, and that ought to be enough to reassure her.   I had to go with Hanakoff.   I have made a success, do you hear ?   Don't worry, don't tremble.   I must find Rosa.   Where is she ?   Rosa !   I've something to tell you !

SACHEL.

No, no; don't speak so loud !

RAFAEL.

Yes, but she does not hear me !   Isn't she in the house ?   Rosa !   What have you said to her ?   Where is she ?   She is not here.   Where is she ?

SACHEL.

Don't ask me, don't ask me !

RAFAEL.

Where is she?

SACHEL.

I couldn't stop her!

RAFAEL.

From what? Where is she?

SACHEL.

Don't know, don't know! She went away!

RAFAEL.

Where—why?

SACHEL.

You shall not blame me! It was not my doing.
Aaron—Aaron—it was he who bribed the postman!
Before God it was not I!

RAFAEL.

Bribed the postman? She did not hear from me?
Where is my wife?

SACHEL.

No, no, Rafael, my boy; my dearest boy—she's
gone, she took money, she deserted you!

RAFAEL.

You are lying !

[*People collect, looking over the canal wall.*

SACHEL.

She said—she said she hated our race—she hated you—she hated all of us ; she was going away, out of the Ghetto, away, off there, there— [*He points away from the canal. The excitement at the canal wall increases. RAFAEL starts as if towards the wall.*] Not there, not there, Rafael, my boy, my boy !

RAFAEL.

What's the matter down there ? [*Two men bring ROSA up the steps ; the crowd obscures her from RAFAEL.*] Who is that ? My God ! Is it a woman ?

A MAN.

Yes.

RAFAEL.

[*Pushes through the crowd.*] Rosa, Rosa—Rosa ! Oh ! oh ! oh !

SACHEL.

Oh, my boy !—oh, my boy ! Rafael ! Rafael ! I couldn't stop her !

RAFAEL.

[*Turning on his father.*] Ugh! Off from me—off! Oh, oh, damnable, damnable monster! Take him away!

AN OLD MAN.

He's your father! Shame! shame!
[*Hisses from crowd.*

RAFAEL.

[*To* SACHEL.] Keep your cursed talons off! Murderer! Murderer! You made her drown herself!

A SECOND MAN.

Leave him alone! Shame! This is the man who blasphemes God!

A THIRD MAN.

He profaned the synagogue—he curses his father!
[RAFAEL *meanwhile looks upon the body of* ROSA.

THE SECOND MAN.

Shall he do all this—this—in our teeth? [*Hisses from the crowd.*] Hide your face! Hide your face!
[*Advances on* RAFAEL.

RAFAEL.

Stand away from her! [*Throws him down, turns to his father.*] O God, if I had not concealed your knavery from her, your holiest oath would not have moved her! And now must you live on, while she lies thus?

SACHEL.

[*To the crowd.*] She poisoned my son; she took away his religion—she killed my son's love for his father! She deserves it—she deserves it!

RAFAEL.

Rosa, my Rosa, you shall not die! Life, life, free-dom—the blue sweet sky, we two together singing in the sun—not the dead soul sighing through the trees —not the whisper of night—the sorrowful shade that passes in the mist! No, no, you must feel my breath upon your cheek, you must feel my arms, you must live, live! [ROSA *stirs.*] Live! She breathes—she breathes! Air—distance—distance, I say! Rosa, it is I, Rafael! You are safe! Not all the fiends in God's grey world· shall thrust an arm between us. Rosa! Rosa!

ROSA.

[*Raising her head a little.*] Rafael, forgive me——

SACHEL.

Rafael—Rafael—she means me.   Forgive *me*—for God's sake—[*on his knees to* RAFAEL, *who turns his back*]—Rafael!

SECOND MAN.

Shame! shame!   He hates his father!

THE CROWD.

Shame! shame!   Punish him!

     [*The crowd closes in on* RAFAEL.

ROSA.

[*In fear.*] Rafael!

RAFAEL.

Are you no better than a mob of Christians? Stand back!   [*Pushes the crowd back violently.*] Rosa, Rosa—away—out of the Ghetto—into the air! Rosa!

    [*The crowd starts to close in again; he takes*
     ROSA *in his arms and rushes across the*
     bridge.   The crowd follows, walking rapidly.
     SACHEL *is left solitary.*

SACHEL.

Rafael!   Raf——   [*He falls.*

Enter A WATCHMAN.

WATCHMAN.

Eleven o'clock, and all's— [*Stops and looks at* SACHEL, *who stirs and sobs.*] Eleven o'clock!

[*Exit* WATCHMAN, *thoughtfully.*

Eleven o'clock !

THE END,

Printed by BALLANTYNE, HANSON &- Co.
London &- Edinburgh

www.ingramcontent.com/pod-product-compliance
Lightning Source LLC
Chambersburg PA
CBHW030902050726
47500CB00009B/981